A TOUCH *of* HOMICIDE

PETER S. FISCHER

www.petersfischer.com

Also By Peter S. Fischer

Me and Murder, She Wrote
Expendable: A Tale of Love and War
The Blood of Tyrants
The Terror of Tyrants

The Hollywood Murder Mystery Series

Jezebel in Blue Satin
We Don't Need No Stinking Badges
Love Has Nothing to Do With It
Everybody Wants An Oscar
The Unkindness of Strangers
Nice Guys Finish Dead
Pray For Us Sinners
Has Anybody Here Seen Wyckham?
Eyewitness to Murder
A Deadly Shoot in Texas
Everybody Let's Rock
A Touch of Homicide
Some Like 'Em Dead
Dead Men Pay No Debts
The Death of Her Yet
Dead and Buried

ISBN 978-1523350728

To Barry Diller and Aaron Spelling...
who many years ago took a chance
on a complete nobody.

PROLOGUE

I am sitting in a darkened projection room at a studio which shall remain unnamed watching a British-made film which should also be unnamed but is in actuality called "Death on the Cotswolds". Someday soon it will be foisted upon an unsuspecting American public and promoted as the new breakout hit of 1957. It deserves to have unanimous pans but there are always one or two newspaper critics from places like Saskatoon or Yellow Knife or Upper Beardsley Township who will find some speck of watchability to recommend it and this mention will be taken out of context and the writer of this review will find his or her name prominently displayed in ads which will appear in the *New York Times* and hundreds of other papers all over the country. It's one of the ways the business works and not much can be done about it. I should know. I am a publicity man for filmdom and in the past I have been guilty of just such a scam.

My name is Joe Bernardi and I am a partner in Bowles & Bernardi, a management and publicity firm among the most successful in the motion picture industry. My partner is Bertha Bowles, a brassy bright babe of considerable years, who is the best at what she does. She manages careers. I publicize them. I also publicize motion pictures but that's a whole different story.

I am here because Bertha asked me to be here. She is carefully watching and evaluating the performance of a fresh new actress named Jill Haworth, age 14, with no other credits, newly minted from the prestigious Corona Stage School in Great Britain. Her part is small but showy and pivotal to the plot. If Bertha likes what she sees we may take on Miss Haworth for a possible film career here in the states. For Bertha I will do just about anything but this is too much. Maybe if I had a bag of popcorn to dig into it wouldn't seem as bad. Maybe not.

I wiggle my ass to get more comfortable but it doesn't help as I try to recap the storyline in my mind. Lord Whozimacallit is found dead in the study of his baronial estate in the countryside by the head housekeeper, Patience Ratchet, who screams at top volume attracting the other members of the household. His wife Beatrice is first on the scene and faints dead away at the sight of his body, overcome with grief. We shall learn that Beatrice has been trying to divorce the old bastard for a year and was threatened with poverty if she set one foot outside of the manor door. The Lord's youngest son Rodney is equally devastated but thankful that the old boy expired before he was able to change his will which he was in the process of doing. Rodney's wife Penelope, a social climbing bitch, is equally pleased by this turn of events. Only the Lord's sweet and loving niece, Hyacinth (Jill Haworth) seems genuinely saddened by the old man's death. The Lord's older son, Edgar, heir to the title of Viscount of Backwater, arrives from London midway through the film. He can't possibly be a suspect. Or can he? Not really except that the old Lord was secretly sleeping with Edgar's young wife, Vivien, because Edgar had lost interest in her, possibly because he felt that he had found true love in the arms of Charles Cavendish, a junior clerk in the law firm retained by the family. Charles has accompanied Edgar and Vivien to the manor for the weekend, ostensibly on business. But perhaps not. Visiting the manor this fateful weekend are American director Drake Mallard and his mistress, famed actress Gloria Grace who has just undergone an abortion and also had a face lift, not, presumably, at the same time. Mallard was defamed by the Lord's newspaper and is here at the manor to negotiate a settlement in a million pound lawsuit. He has been accompanied by his London solicitor, Bryan

Polsby, a diehard professional adversary of Charles Cavendish, and who was secretly a spy for the Nazis during World War Two and now aspires to a seat in Commons from which he someday hopes to claim the Prime Ministership. Tending to the property is landscaper Nils Forsberg, son of the partner the old guy cheated four decades ago to gain control of the newspaper empire. He is in love with an upstairs maid named Pansy Plimpton who has been working for the Lord for several months and is, unknown to the others, the Lord's illegitimate daughter from a liaison prior to the war with a Russian ballerina named Sonya Voscayovich. There are other complications but they are minor.

My head is reeling. A dozen suspects and every one of them with a 24 karat motive to kill the despotic bastard. I don't know who the writer is but I suspect he was sniffing airplane glue during the entire time he was committing this monstrosity to paper. But wait, it gets worse. As we near the denouement, Chief Inspector Folderol, or whatever his name is, has gathered all of the suspects into the study which should have created a problem since there are a dozen of them and only three chairs but never mind. For this scene nine heretofore unknown chairs have suddenly materialized. Now I don't really give a damn who the killer is. I just want this movie over with but no, this poppinjay of a policeman must now strut about the room, thrusting fingers at various individuals, spouting all sorts of hypotheses and conjectures giving the actual killer a chance to escape justice by dying of old age. If this arrant nonsense is supposed to pass for reality then I am Harpo Marx.

Finally the film ends and the lights come up. Bertha looks over at me.

"Well?" she says.

"Well what?" I growl irritably.

"I grant you the film has problems," Bertha says.

"You think?"

"These British drawing room mysteries do poorly in America. It will come and go in the wink of an eyelash."

"Pity the public if it takes that long," I say.

"What did you think of Jill?"

"Cute. Perky. Talented."

"I agree," Bertha says.

"If they burn the negative and all the prints she might have a future."

By now we are walking out of the projection building and heading for my car. She no longer drives. Her eyes are quitting on her.

"It wasn't that bad," she says.

"No?" I protest in high dudgeon. "With a couple of exceptions the actors reached a level heretofore only seen in a Three Stooges two-reeler. The writer, whose name I thankfully did not catch, concocted a story so far removed from reality that it would have made Jules Verne proud. One coincidence after another. Concoction upon concoction."

"It's the genre," she says. "Very stylized."

"Stylized, my ass, Bert. It was total bullshit."

I open the car door for her and she slides into the passenger seat. I come around and get behind the wheel.

"I'm sorry I spoiled your day, Joe."

"Not my day, Bert. Just two hours of it. Now you and I will hop over to Musso's for lunch, I'll down three ice cold Coors to go with my New York steak and by two o'clock I will have forgotten all about "Death on the Cotswolds".

Oh, and by the way, for those who should know better but don't, and spend good money to view this train wreck, the killer is Patience Ratchet, the housekeeper who discovered the body. Why she did it I do not know because the writer never divulged her motive.

Like I said, genre, my ass.

CHAPTER ONE

Five days have passed since we screened "that picture". I'm over it, I think. Bertha is waiting to hear from Jill Haworth's people in London. Meanwhile we are tooling along Santa Monica Boulevard on our way to the Fox studios. I'm driving. Bertha is talking.

Actually she is muttering under her breath and I am getting every third or fourth word. None of it is pleasant and a high percentage of it is profanity. All of it concerns Diane Varsi, an aspiring actress whom we represent. She is very young. She is also very lucky. Following a breakthrough role in the film 'Peyton Place', she has been cast as Gary Cooper's daughter in 20th Century Fox's production of 'Ten North Frederick' which is where we are headed. Diane is in her dressing room and refuses to come out. Neither Bertha nor I know the reason for this behavior. It is certainly not professional but at the age of 19 in her second motion picture role, maybe she doesn't yet know the rules. Or maybe the adulation and awards that 'Peyton Place' brought her have turned her into a teenaged diva. We shall see.

I drive up to the main gate and give my name. The security guard has been expecting us. He gives me directions to the sound stage. Park anywhere, he tells us. He will phone the set and notify Mr.

Brackett that we are on the way. Charlie Brackett is the producer. At 66 he's already a Hollywood legend with three Oscars to his credit and I can only imagine what he must think of Diane Varsi.

Even as I park the car Brackett is emerging from the sound stage and hurries to Bertha, embracing her warmly. The embrace lasts a smidgen longer than propriety might suggest and I wonder if Bertha, whose romantic liaisons over the past thirty years are legendary, might have had a fleeting relationship with this distinguished gentleman. But then I recall that Brackett had a long and happy marriage before he was widowed and then went ahead and married his dead wife's sister. In Brackett's case I think I give Bertha too much credit.

Brackett gives me a welcoming hello and the three of us enter the sound stage which is eerily quiet. Phil Dunne, the director, is sitting in his chair studying his script. He obviously wants no part of Varsi. The rest of the crew is standing around with nothing to do and no place to go. Varsi may emerge ready to work in the next five minutes or she may still be ensconced in her trailer two hours from now. Like the Army, movie making is often a hurry-up-and-wait kind of business.

Bertha and Brackett scurry over to the far side of the sound stage where Varsi's trailer is parked. I opt for the craft services table and a hot cup of coffee. I could also use a bite to eat and I am carefully surveying the baked goods when I hear a familiar voice.

"Stay away from the doughnuts."

I look off to my right where Coop is stretched out in his chair, a fedora pulled down over his eyes as if sleeping. He tips back his hat and looks at me with a smile.

"Hard as rocks and totally indigestible," he says.

"I'll take your word for it, Coop." I say.

Gary Cooper hefts himself out of his chair and stretches. The face is the same, the smile just as shy and warm as it ever was, but he looks thinner. Maybe even frail. The weight loss doesn't look good on a man as active and robust as Cooper who has spent a career being a man of action. I've heard the rumors of ill health. I hope they're not true but the evidence is staring me in the face.

He reaches out and shakes my hand.

"How've you been, Joe? It's been a while."

"At least a year and I'm fine. How's the picture going?"

"All right I guess," Cooper says with a glance in the direction of Varsi's trailer. "I wonder if Tracy knew what was coming?"

Spencer Tracy had been signed to play the lead but bowed out several weeks ago for reasons still not clear. Cooper was signed to replace him.

"What's she like?" I ask. I've only met Varsi twice and then only briefly.

"The kid? She's okay. Very talented. A little quirky. What's the term? A flake. Pleasant enough but sometimes I think she's off visiting her own planet."

"What's her beef this morning?" I ask.

He smiles, shaking his head.

"To tell you the truth, Joe, I have no idea." He glances at his watch. "I think I'd better call Rocky and tell her I may be real late for dinner. I'll see you around."

He walks off toward his dressing room. Rocky is his wife of twenty-five years except for a brief separation a few years back. Cooper's reputation as a ladies man is legendary but most people agree that Rocky,forgiving and forbearing, is the anchor that keeps him grounded. I doubt he'd argue.

I hang around for a few more minutes before I decide to take my coffee and go outside to get some sun and fresh air. It's a gorgeous early November day in Southern California, not a cloud in the sky and a temperature in the low 70's. Much too nice a day to spend in a dark cavernous sound stage playing nursemaid to a pampered starlet barely out of high school.

"Yo!"

I look off to my left and see a man hurrying toward me. He looks young and the closer he gets, the younger he looks. Decked out in grey flannel with a red striped power tie, he seems just like the hundreds of other wannabes running around the studios looking for a toehold that will turn them from also rans into actual players.

Out of breath, the newcomer reaches me, hand outstretched.

"Joe Bernardi. My gosh, I can't believe I'm actually meeting you. What a privilege. Avery Sterling."

I take his hand. We shake. But I am wary. I am seldom buttered up so blatantly and when I am it pays to check for my watch, my wallet and my cuff links.

"How do you do," I say by way of being polite.

"Doing well, thanks. Just had a great meeting with Mitzi Gaynor. She's pretty much set for my next film. What a gal. She's got it all. Oh, excuse me." He reaches in a shirt pocket and produces a business card which he hands me. I scan it. Crown Sterling Productions. Avery Sterling, President. It also lists a phone number and a street address. I've never heard of this guy or his company which is not surprising. As I said, Hollywood does not suffer from a shortage of wannabes.

I start to hand back the card. He shrugs.

"Keep it," he says. I'm glad to see he has more than one.

"Here's the thing, Joe," he says. "You don't mind if I call you Joe." Actually I do. "I'm going to need you and Bertha on my side when I get close to a release date but it won't hurt to bring you into the picture as early as possible, am I right?"

"Well," I say, "we're a little overloaded just now, Mr. Sterling—"

"Avery. Call me Avery."

"Avery. And we're not taking on any new clients at this time."

"Sure, I get it," he says without blinking an eye, "but when I get through telling you about this property I've optioned, I think you will definitely reconsider."

I look past him and see Bertha emerging from the sound stage on Brackett's arm. I start around the car to open the door for her.

"Sorry," I say to Sterling, "Maybe at some later date."

"All I need is a few minutes of your time," he says, almost whining.

"Call my secretary and make an appointment," I tell him. I turn my attention to Bertha. "Everything okay?"

"For the moment," she says drily, giving Brackett a hug and an air kiss. A few moments later I am backing out of my parking spot, narrowly missing Avery Sterling who is still trying to engage me in conversation. We speed away and turn onto Santa Monica Boulevard.

"Who was the slick item in the three piece suit?" she asks.

"The next Zanuck."

"Which one?" she asks. "Darryl or Elmo?"

I laugh. One look and Bertha had him pegged.

"You hungry?" I ask. "It's lunchtime."

"I could eat," she says.

I drive us to Wang's which is a couple of blocks from the office. It's a hole in the wall but the food is terrific and because it looks like a roach-infested dump, it's never crowded. Wang is a great cook but he's a lousy businessman. We feel guilty not wising him up but we're afraid if we do, the place will get so crowded we'll never get a table. Over dim sum and chow mein we discuss Diane Varsi. Bertha was able to get her back in front of the camera but it's only a matter of time before she's at it again. She's not a bad sort, Bertha tells me, and there's nothing cruel or mean in her make up, she's just plain scared. The fame and the money and the responsibility have all come too fast and she doesn't know how to handle it. Bertha thinks she'll grow out of it. I hope she's right.

We get back to the office shortly after two and there, waiting for me in our reception area, is Avery Sterling. He smiles broadly and stands as we enter. I'm sure that my expression is not one of welcome but he manages to ignore it as he approaches. Bertha keeps moving. She wants no part of this.

"I tried to take your advice, Joe, but your girl wouldn't make an appointment for me so I thought I'd wait for The Man himself."

I glance at my watch.

"I'm sorry, Mr. Sterling, but this isn't a good time. I have a very important two-thirty."

His eyes flick to the wall clock which reads 2:08. He reaches in his pocket and hands me a folded note. I unfold it. It's not a note, it's a check for $1000.

"I need fifteen minutes of your time and I'm willing to pay for it," he says. "Please." He has a very hopeful look in his eyes.

"What's it about?" I ask.

"Orson Welles," he says. "He needs your help."

CHAPTER TWO

I'm hooked.

Orson Welles is one of my heroes and has been since the first time I saw 'Citizen Kane' in a tiny little theater on Main Street in the dinky metropolis of Oolagha, Oklahoma. Marcie Lou Futterman and I were seated in the back row of the balcony sharing a bag of popcorn. She was all over me like marinara on linguini looking for action and for the first time in months I was ignoring her and concentrating on the search for 'rosebud'. At first it was her tongue in my ear and finally her hand down my pants playing with Little Joey. When I finally realized what she was up to I said something rude. She said something rude in return and dumped the popcorn in my lap as she stood and marched resolutely toward the staircase leading to the lobby. I did not follow. My eyes never left the screen and I never saw Marcie Lou again. No loss.

I gesture to the chair opposite my desk and Avery Sterling sits.

"All right," I say, handing him his check back, "I'm listening. How can I help Mr. Welles?"

"What do you know about 'Touch of Evil'?" Sterling asks me.

"It's a movie Mr. Welles directed in Tijuana. He also acted in it along with Charlton Heston and Janet Leigh and I hear it's not very good."

"Well, you're wrong, Joe. It's very good. World class good and by the way, Orson couldn't get permission to shoot across the border. It was shot in Venice." He doesn't add 'dummy' but that's what he means. It's the way the kid puts me down that makes me like him even less than I did five minutes ago.

"If the picture is so good why is Universal-International re-cutting it?" I ask.

"Because U-I makes movies for people who don't like to stand in line. Francis the Talking Mule, Ma and Pa Kettle, and who's their biggest star? Audie Murphy who's even shorter than Alan Ladd. Gimmee a break."

"You exaggerate."

"They haven't won a Best Picture Oscar in twenty-eight years and don't tell me 'Hamlet' which was a Rank film for Two Cities. When a performer gets a nomination in a U-I film it's a banner headline in 'Variety'. Those are the people who are recutting Mr. Welles' masterpiece."

This guy is an opinionated little snot but I don't throw him out of the office because I remain curious as to why Welles needs my help.

"Masterpiece. That's a strong word."

"I can prove it," Sterling says. "I have a copy of the first cut."

I sit up a little straighter.

"You have Orson Welles' first cut of the picture?"

"109 minutes and it's brilliant," he continues.

"Where'd you get it?"

"I didn't steal it if that's what you mean," Sterling says. "Would you like to see it?"

Would I? Would I also like to find a naked Ava Gardner wrapped in clear cellophane under my Christmas tree?

"When?" I ask.

Sterling looks at his watch.

"How about four o'clock? My offices."

Is this guy for real? Every bone in my body says no but if he has a copy of Welles' first cut of 'Touch of Evil', then I could be all wrong about him.

"I take my coffee with cream and two sugars and hold the popcorn," I say with a smile. The kid smiles back.

Four o'clock rolls around and I find myself walking into the lobby of a new office building on Crenshaw Boulevard just south of Santa Monica. There is a reception desk but at the moment, no receptionist. I check the directory next to the elevators. Half the offices are available for lease but Suite 2 on the third floor has been rented out to Crown Sterling Productions. If this guy is a phony, he is a first class phony with all the trappings. I get on the elevator and push the button for '3' and when I get off, the first thing I see is a set of double doors with raised brass lettering: Crown Sterling Productions, Film and Television Production and Marketing, Avery Sterling, President. The only thing missing is the kid's picture. When I open the door and step inside I realize I needn't have worried. A six foot tall photo of Avery dominates the wall to my left. He is smiling as if amused by an inside joke.

The thickly carpeted foyer features potted plants, sleek and expensive modern furniture as well as a massive reception desk but like downstairs, no receptionist. Just then Sterling emerges from one of the offices and greets me warmly, apologizing for the absence of the receptionist. She's an aspiring actress and had a cattle call at three o'clock. A cattle call is only slightly less crowded than a Shriner's convention. Dozens of aspiring young actresses jam into an office for a chance at thirty seconds with either a casting director or perhaps even the director. Short of stripping naked, none will make an impression and eventually the director will give the part to his girlfriend which was the whole idea in the first place.

"Hey, how do you like the digs?" he asks. "Not bad, huh?" He grins like a kid let loose in a candy store with a five dollar bill.

"Come on, let me show you around."

He leads me down a short corridor and pokes his head into the first doorway.

"Roy, say hello to Joe Bernardi. Bowles & Bernardi. Joe's here to see the Welles cut."

Roy waves 'hi' from his desk which displays a lot of paperwork and a calculator. Sterling explains that Roy Watson is the company business manager and handles all the finances and contracts. He's young with a buzz cut and a bow tie. My guess is he's just out of film school and is probably younger than Sterling.

In the next office I meet an older man wearing suspenders, sitting at his desk, feet up, reading a script. Another dozen or so are piled on the edge of his desk. His name is Walker and he's in charge of acquisitions. His face seems familiar but I can't place him.

"I know you," I say.

"I don't think so," Walker replies.

"Are you sure? Friar's Club? The Academy?"

"Sorry," he smiles. "I'm really not in the business. Just an ex-college professor trying to pick up a few bucks waiting for my next job."

I smile. "Well, nice to meet you," I tell him, still not convinced. His face is too familiar and I haven't been within spitting distance of a college classroom in twenty years.

We exchange a couple more pleasantries and then Sterling and I head for a door at the end of the hallway. It opens into a conference room which has been set up for the screening. The projector sits on the long oak conference table facing a temporary screen standing near the far wall. The projectionist is introduced to me. His name is Ralph. He's pudgy, balding, eager to please. Also on the table is a coffee set up next to a comfortable padded chair. Sterling gestures for me to sit and slips into the chair next to me.

"Whenever you're ready, Joe," Sterling says.

"I'm ready," I say, fixing my coffee.

The lights go dim and Ralph starts the projector. There are no opening credits. The picture jumps onto the screen. A warehouse area near the waterfront. We catch sight of a car. The camera follows it down a long street, then continues to follow as it makes a turn and then another one, The camera starts to move, tracking the car as it speeds along, moving closer but continuing to track. I keep waiting for a close cut to the car. It never comes. Welles has shot this opening sequence in "One". An uncut continuous master that seems to go on forever and then, just when you think it can't continue, the car suddenly explodes into a fireball lighting the night sky. I'm transfixed. What I have just seen is pure Orsonian genius. I have been grabbed by this opening shot. I will watch the rest of the movie continually in Welles's grasp. There is no music, few sound effects, garbled dialogue. Technically it is a mess. Creatively it is sheer genius. After one hundred and nine minutes, the film ends and the lights come up.

For a moment I say nothing and then I look over at Sterling.

"Where did you get this?" I demand to know.

"It's not important," Sterling says.

"It is to me. You're trying to get me involved in something here. I'm not sure what. But I am damned sure I don't want to get sucked into something that sounds even remotely unethical."

Sterling shakes his head violently.

"This is all on the up and up, I swear," he says. "What did you think of the picture?"

"It's brilliant, obviously," I say. "Where did you get the print?"

"I told you, I didn't steal it."

I get to my feet.

"Not good enough, Mr. Sterling. Thank you for allowing me to view it. I wish you luck in whatever you are up to but you do it without me."

I head for the door. Sterling calls after me.

"Wait!"

I turn at the door.

"I'm waiting," I say.

"Let's talk in my office," he says moving past me and opening the door. I hold my ground. "Please," he says.

I hesitate, then relent. His expression is desperate and my curiosity is getting the better of me.

Avery Sterling's office is ostentatious, just what I would expect from an ambitious young pischer with delusions of acceptance and success. His desk is mammoth and slightly elevated. The carpeting, like the carpeting in the foyer, is extra thick and deep. Several bookcases line the walls. The shelves are mostly empty. The rest of the wall space is taken up with posters of movies none of which he produced. There is one photograph in the room. It sits in a standup frame in the middle of the coffee table. Otherwise, the office is cold and sterile like the rest of the suite. It is an office complex that could have been created by one of MGM's top set designers, slick and costly and just as empty of reality. I move closer to the coffee table to check out the framed photo. Two men. One is Avery. He and an older man are smiling for the camera, arms about each other's shoulders. I've seen the old man somewhere before but I can't place him.

"My father," Sterling says, looking over my shoulder.

"His face seems familiar," I say.

"It should. It's plastered all over your TV set seven nights a week."

I look again and it comes to me.

"Jake Silver."

Sterling nods. "Dear old Dad," he says with something of an edge.

Jake Silver owns a chain of low end jewelry stores from San Diego north to San Francisco. He stars in his own commercials, usually with a jeweler's loupe in his eye. Everyday is bargain day at Silver's where credit is extended to anyone with a pulse. A born hustler, he is a millionaire many times over but in contrast to his high-pressure carny personna as seen on television, he is regarded as a quiet spoken civic leader deeply involved in charities ranging from B'hai Brith to the local United Way and St. Elizabeth's Shelter for Homeless Women.

"Silver? Sterling?" I ask curiously as I move to a nearby sofa and sit.

"I was born Avrom Silverstein. Great name for a rabbi. Not so good for a movie mogul."

I wave my arm around.

"And all this? I assume your Dad's a silent partner."

He chooses to ignore my supposition.

"You asked about the rough cut. I'll tell you about it. Orson started cutting the picture with an editor named Curtiss but they had wildly different ideas on what the picture should look like so Curtiss was fired and Virgil Vogel brought in. They worked together perfectly. Ralph— our projectionist Ralph Cacavas— was the assistant editor. They started in April and finished the first cut in July. That's when Vogel asked Orson if he wanted to have a second copy run off as a matter of protection in case something happened to the original. Orson felt it wasn't necessary but Vogel was not so sure knowing how Universal-International sometimes worked after a director had given up his film. Anyway, unknown to Orson, Vogel made a second copy of the cut and gave it to Ralph to put in a safe place, just in case. Orson went off on another project and the film was put into the hands of a U-I staff editor named Stell. A couple of new scenes were written and shot and incorporated into the cut even as a lot of Orson's footage was being sliced out. Orson returned from overseas last week and was shown the new version. He was appalled and said so. In his words, it is abysmal. Fearing that Orson was going to cause trouble, someone at the studio has started a low key campaign through the press to discredit Orson and his work."

"And that's where I come in," I say.

"That's right," Sterling says. "If anyone can negate the effects of this vicious whispering campaign, it's you."

"And Mr. Welles concurs?"

"Naturally."

"And what's in this for you, Mr. Sterling?" I ask.

"Simple, Joe. I have a script ready to go. I want Orson to direct it. I feel if I help him out with this problem, I have a good chance of signing him."

I hesitate. The kid is good. He's articulate and he knows how to sell a point but I think he's wrong. Wrong about me and almost certainly wrong about Orson Welles. I'll try to let him down softly,

"I'm sorry, Avery." I say, "but I really can't help you. This is shaping up to be a legal fight between Universal and Mr. Welles and I want no part of it. I think maybe he would be better off retaining a lawyer though I have no idea what his legal position is."

"You're wrong, Joe."

I get to my feet, "Well, maybe so, but that's how I feel. Thanks for letting me see the film. Tell Mr. Welles how much I enjoyed watching it."

As I go to the door, I hear him scream at me.

"Don't you turn your back on me, you bastard!"

I turn back to him in disbelief.

"What did you say?"

His face has turned pink and his eyes are wild.

"You heard me! You're nothing, Bernardi! I don't need you, you high and mighty son of a bitch!"

"Hey, watch your mouth!" I shout back.

"You want to do something about it?" he sneers, stepping toward me.

"What's the matter with you, kid? You want to fight me?"

"I could wipe up the floor with you, old timer," he says.

"Maybe you could," I say. "You could also try to produce movies from a jail cell. Let me tell you something, buster. You had better learn to keep that temper of yours under control. There are people in this town, if you talk to them like that, they'll shut you up permanently."

"And I suppose you're one of them," Sterling says.

"Don't tempt me. It would be a pleasure," I say as I turn and head out the door, nearly bowling over Ralph Cacavas, the projectionist, who has been standing there, mouth agape, taking it all in. As I move quickly down the corridor heading toward the elevators, I can hear more screaming but it doesn't register. I am well out of any possible relationship with this egotistical loon. I can't believe that Welles has anything to do with him.

The elevator door opens and I start to step in just as a dervish in a mink coat charges out of the cab and nearly bowls me over. She's an attractive blonde wearing gold and diamond earrings the size of silver dollars and the expression on her face tells me her mood is lousy. Even though it's not my fault, I apologize. She seems not to hear as she marches across the hallway to Avery Sterling's offices.

As I redeem my car from a nearby parking lot I remember that I have a seven o'clock dinner date tonight with Bertha at Scandia's. We are wining and dining a client and good friend, Tony Randall, who will be leaving shortly for New York to start rehearsals for "Oh, Captain" a musical comedy based on an old Alec Guiness movie called "The Captain's Paradise". My watch reads six-fifteen. Too late to go home or to the office so I decide to go straight to the restaurant and grab a quick drink at the bar.

Fifteen minutes later I pull up to the entrance and hand my car over to the valet. It's early on a Tuesday evening and the place isn't crowded. I double check to make sure the reservation has been made (it has) and then I wander into the bar which is equally unpopulated. I am about to slip onto a stool at the end of the bar when my eye is caught by a gentleman sitting alone at a small table along the far wall. He is large of frame and wearing horn-rimmed glasses as he pores over a piece of paper in his left hand while his right hand lifts a wine glass filled with a rich red to his lips. I have never met him but there is no doubt about who I am looking at. At age 38 I am about to meet my lifelong idol, Orson Welles.

CHAPTER THREE

"Mr. Welles?" I say.

He looks up, peering at me over the top of those horn-rimmed frames.

"Yes?" he says in that deep syrupy baritone.

I put out my hand.

"I apologize for intruding. Joe Bernardi. Bowles & Bernardi. We've never met but my partner talks about you so often I feel as if I know you."

Welles smiles as we shake hands

"And Bertha returns the compliment when she talks about you, Mr. Bernardi." He gestures. "Please. Sit down. Join me for a glass of wine."

"No, I don't want to interrupt."

"Don't be ridiculous." He waves to the bartender. "Phillipe, another glass!" The bartender nods. I pull up a chair. Welles has a nearly full bottle of a French Cabernet Sauvignon at his elbow. I know nothing about wine, imported or domestic, but I am sure this is a fine label. Orson Welles does not settle for second best in anything, even when he doesn't have a dime to his name.

"And how is dear Bertha? I haven't spoken to her in months," Welles says.

“Feeling well, prospering, and as pugnacious as ever,” I tell him.

He laughs.

“Good for her. You know, there was a time when I thought that artist management was a parasitic profession but the more I see of these youngsters coming up from regional theater and television, the more I realize they haven’t got a clue about how to build and maintain a career.”

“True enough, Mr. Welles,” I say.

“Please. Make that Orson. Now and then I take the time to spend an hour or two with kids in film schools and that’s all I hear, Mr. Welles this, Mr. Welles that. I feel old and passe, revered beyond reason like some doddering old archbishop. My God, Joe, I’m only 43 and they treat me like their grandfathers.”

“Can’t sympathize,” I say. “I’m not there yet.”

Phillipe, the bartender, brings over the fresh glass and Orson does the honors. I take a sip. It is tasty and mellow. I smile appreciatively.

“A votre sante,” I say taking a healthier swallow. Orson joins me.

“The reason I stopped by, “ I say, “I wanted to tell you how much I enjoyed ‘Touch of Evil’. It’s brilliant. I mean that sincerely.”

Orson frowns.

“Thank you, Joe, but you must tell me how and where you saw it.”

“I got a special screening from Avery Sterling at his offices.”

“Who?”

Warning bells suddenly start to clang in my head. It’s that blank look on Orson’s face. He has no clue as to who I am discussing.

“Avery Sterling. Ambitious young producer, early 20’s, slick dresser, spouts a load of bullshit that would make a politician proud.”

Slowly Orson nods as the situation comes into focus.

“Ah, yes. That one. The young hustler with the so-called second copy of my initial cut."

"Not so-called, Orson. I watched it. Just short of two hours long and as I said, brilliant."

He drums his fingers on the table.

"I told Virgil I wanted no second copy laying around. Damn it." He shakes his head and lets out a sigh. "I suppose I should be angry," he says, "and in a sense I am. Perhaps I should also be grateful given the situation that has arisen with Universal."

"Then they've re-cut the picture," I say.

"Re-cut? Yes, Joe, I suppose a moderate man might make such a judgement. In my opinion they have slashed it into ribbons, turning it into a monstrosity that only barely resembles a motion picture. If and when they release it in that condition, my once proud reputation, now a shadow of its former luster, will further turn me into an industry joke. The boy wonder is no more and the only wonder that survives is the wonder people have that I am still around."

"That bad?"

"That bad," he says.

"And you have no recourse?"

"None legally. Deja vu, Joe. Deja vu." He takes a deep swallow from his glass and stares off into space.

"The Ambersons," I say.

"Yes, the Ambersons, recreated into something not quite magnificent." He's talking about 'The Magnificent Ambersons', his followup film to 'Citizen Kane'. "I handed the film over to RKO and went off to Brazil to work on this film as a favor to Nelson Rockefeller. When I returned to the states, I found my film had been seriously mugged by a gang of ham-handed editors. I protested in vain but as part of a renegotiation of my contract I'd given up final cut on the picture. A huge mistake, one I've always regretted."

"And now it's happening all over again," I say.

"It is," Orson says. "I have sent them a fifty-eight page memo outlining exactly how 'Touch of Evil' should be cut. Any fool could follow my instructions but I very much fear my memo will be ignored. The picture will appear and disappear in a matter of days. The studio executive who green lighted the picture may or may not be fired and once again that old stumblebum Welles will be unable to find work as a director or raise money for any of his ambitious projects."

"I think you exaggerate," I say.

"Do I? It took me two years to complete 'Othello'. Stop, start, stop, start again. Begging for money like a one-legged mendicant, finally finishing and then taking another three years before I could get it released. Hollywood perceives me with suspicious eyes, Joe. Where once they saw boundless talent, they now see a pompous egomaniac desperately trying to recapture the adulation engendered by his first big success."

"That's not true," I say.

"No?" Orson says. "I wonder."

He lifts his glass and takes another deep swallow of wine.

"How did you get involved with Avery Sterling?" I ask.

Orson nods.

"How indeed. It's coming back to me now. He accosted me coming out of the Friar's Club about two weeks ago after my luncheon with Bob Hope and Danny Kaye. This young man, Mr. Sterling, lathered me up with all sorts of praise for the picture and I believe he did mention something about a second copy of my cut. Of course, I didn't believe him. He talked about the backbiting that was coming from some of the Universal people and said he knew just the person who could do something about it. I didn't believe that either but I am waiting for the valet to bring my car and I can't politely get away from him so I nod and smile a lot. He tells me he has a first rate script that needs a page one rewrite and he will also need a director and beyond that, I would be perfect casting as the diabolical villain. At that moment the valet drives up with my car and I am spared any further discourse with the gentleman. I haven't seen or heard from him since."

"Well, beware, Orson. He's out there and he has his sights set on you."

"And you as well, Joe," Orson says with a smile. He reaches for the bottle to refill my glass but I wave him off as I check my watch which now reads seven o'clock. I get to my feet.

"I'd love to stay. This has been really enjoyable. But I'm due in the other room. Bertha and I are dining with Tony Randall. In fact we'd be delighted if you'd join us."

"Most gracious, Joe, but I am expecting company. A wealthy wheat farmer from Kansas who has fantasies of becoming a motion picture mogul. I will do my best to encourage him in this pipe dream."

He puts out his hand and we shake.

"By the way," I say, "on the chance that Bertha or I need to get in touch, where are you staying?"

He smiles. "Joe Cotten's guest room. The mattress is lumpy but the company is exquisite. He and Lenore are wonderful hosts. I'll be there until Friday when I fly out to the Bahamas for a few days with Mr. Coward which should be entertaining if nothing else."

I agree completely and tell him so and then I turn and head off toward the dining room having spent a short but delightful time with a man who is not only a legend but a warm and personable human being as well.

For the next three hours, Bertha and I are regaled at dinner by Tony Randall who has an endless repertoire of show business stories which he has told and retold many times over. They are always worth hearing again but by ten-thirty my derriere needs relief and Bertha finally calls it a night. We wish Tony a world of success in New York and head for our cars. It's been a long day, mentally exhausting, and all I want to do is curl up under the sheets and zonk out. Realistically I'm looking at another forty-five minutes before I get home to my modest little house in Van Nuys. I like to think of myself as young and vibrant but in reality, middle age seems to have me in its grip and I am not happy about it. Maybe later this week I'll sign up at a gym and start working out. This is a promise I have made to myself on several occasions but I have yet to follow through. I have no reason to think this week will be any different.

I head toward Mulholland Drive where I will cut across the crest of the hills that separate L.A. from the Valley to Van Nuys Boulevard and head north. As I drive I think about Orson Welles and our mutual pest, young Mister Sterling. My annoyance has abated, replaced by a kind of grudging sympathy and maybe even a tinge of admiration. Sterling is trying to make it in the toughest snake pit of them all and I have to admire his nerve and his tenacity. The motion picture business is no place for the faint of heart and for the most part those who succeed have steel in their spines and no shortage of self-confidence. Unfortunately this combination rewards many people with whom you would not willingly spend more than five minutes of your time. America would be shocked to learn just who these unfavored few are but it's not the job of a press agent to tell them. Quite the opposite. Luckily for Bertha and me we are successful enough so that we can pick and choose who we wish to represent. Although I find it unlikely, perhaps someday Avery Sterling may be one of the industry's most successful producers. If so I doubt we'll represent him. It's this kind of freedom that helps me sleep soundly at night.

I turn onto Mulholland Drive and immediately remember how dark this road can be on a moonless night. There are no streetlights and while the road is in good shape, it's wise to hold one's speed down. There are twists and turns that come up suddenly if you're not paying attention. And then, as if on cue, it happens. A huge clunk, the car is jarred and my hands slip momentarily from the wheel. When I manage to regain control, I feel the wobble immediately. One of my tires has gone flat. I ease to the side of the road into a little clearing and cut the engine. My headlights stab straight ahead into the darkness but aside from that I am enveloped in black on all sides. I reach in the glove box for the flashlight.

I get out of the car and inspect the damage. It's not good. The front right hand tire is not only flat, it has come halfway off the rim. With an audible sigh, I walk around to the boot. Did I mention that I drive a seven year old Bentley Mark VI or that last year I was involved in a head-on collision and unwisely decided to go for a repair job instead of buying a new car? Greater love hath no man than mindless loyalty to a beloved automobile. Greater foolishness also applies. For months the car has been nothing but trouble and now this. No question about it. The damned thing is jinxed. Tomorrow it goes. Tonight I fret and fume.

I start to sift through the collected junk in the boot. Old magazines, a couple of blankets, my daughter Yvette's beach paraphernalia, a rusty putter, two empty coke bottles and finally, the spare tire. I search further for the jack which seems to be missing and then I remember it is missing because I had to change a tire at home and I left the jack in the garage. This situation has now escalated from annoyance to irritation and I have no idea what to do next. Since I pulled over no cars have come by. That is worrisome. I am also in a stretch of road where there are no houses which means no phone with which to call Triple A. Add to this the fact that the temperature has dropped into the mid-50's and I am starting to feel the cold. I think about hoofing it but to where? I am not even remotely close to a service station. My best hope is for a Good Samaritan who will recognize my plight and stop to lend a hand. Mitigating against this is the recent spate of phony roadside "breakdowns" that lure passersby into stopping at which point they are robbed at gunpoint as a reward for their unselfish instincts.

Over the next fifteen minutes, four cars come by. None stop. They don't even slow down. Neighbors help neighbors in Cedar Rapids, Iowa. Los Angeles is no Cedar Rapids. Twenty-two minutes have elapsed when lights once again approach. I edge carefully out onto the road and wave hopefully. For a moment I think this one,too, will drive by but no, it slows and comes to a stop. It is a beat-up pick up truck in bad need of a paint job. The driver rolls down his window and looks out.

"Trouble, senor?" he asks.

"Flat tire," I say.

He's an older man with bronze skin and greying hair.

"Do you have a spare?" he asks.

"Yes, but no jack."

He nods and pulls over to the side of the road just behind my car.

He hops down from the truck and introduces himself. His name is Pedro and he is short, wiry and spry. He examines my damage sympathetically and then smiles.

"I do not think this will take long," he says. He goes to his truck and returns with a scissor jack and a X-shaped lug wrench. Despite his optimism it takes a lot longer than he had anticipated. Finding a decent spot to site the jack becomes a major undertaking and once that is finally accomplished, we have a problem removing the lug nuts. British nuts are not the same as Detroit nuts and he finally has to resort to a set of pliers to remove them. A lesser man might become aggravated by this situation but Pedro is given to happy humming. I offer to help but he smiles and refuses. One man working is quick. Two working takes much longer. Between hums, we chat briefly. He is returning home after a week of picking grapes at a vineyard up near Paso Robles. He lives with his wife and three daughters in Pacoima. His wife is a hairdresser and his oldest daughter who just turned sixteen is learning the business.

Finally he stands up, goes to the jack and lowers it. My car is whole again. I check my watch. I have been here well over an hour. I walk Pedro back to his truck and thank him profusely for his help. I try to hand him fifty dollars but he wants no part of it. He did not stop to help me for money, he says. I tell him I know that but if he won't take the money for himself, take it for his girls. Tomorrow a shopping spree at the May Company. New dresses for all of them. I jam the bills into his shirt pocket. He surrenders. His daughters will be very pleased. He gives me several 'muchos gracias' and I put my arms around him and give him an affectionate hug. I wave goodbye as he gets back in his truck and continues on down the road.

Before I start up the car, I walk back along the road to see if I can find what caused the accident. Within fifteen yards, I spot a large rock about the size of a loaf of bread sitting in the middle of the road. I kick it into the ditch to save some other poor soul the same aggravation I suffered. For my trouble, I get a stab of pain in my big toe. This has really become a lousy evening.

By the time I pull into my driveway, it's one-thirty. As I get out of the car I look next door and see my neighbor, Chuck Bledsoe, hauling his garbage cans to curbside. Tomorrow is collection day, something Chuck and I have a habit of forgetting far too often. I wave to him. He waves back sheepishly. I realize he's wearing pajamas and a bathrobe and I wonder if he was already under the covers when he remembered. Thus reminded I tend to my own garbage cans and finally, a few minutes before two o'clock I manage to find my way into bed. I have already disabled the ringer on the telephone and I have not set the alarm clock. In fact I have turned its face to the wall. If I am lucky I will sleep until noon.

CHAPTER FOUR

I don't make it until noon. Not even close. I disabled the phone and ignored the alarm clock but I forgot all about the front doorbell. Now it is ringing like some musical jackhammer—ding-dong, ding-dong—refusing to shut up and driving me mad. I lurch out of bed, glance at the clock which reads 6:45 and stumble out of the bedroom in the direction of the front door. I am wearing a frown and a pair of boxer shorts and nothing else and if Mamie Eisenhower is on the other side of my front door, she's in for an off-putting surprise.

I yank the door open and find myself staring into the face of my good friend, Aaron Kleinschmidt, Detective Lieutenant, Los Angeles Homicide. His eyes lower to take in my shorts and a smile crosses his face.

"Cute. Very cute," he says.

I look down and realize I am wearing my Cupid boxers, a Valentine's Day present from Bunny several years ago when she was at her horniest.

"If you prefer I'll take them off," I say.

"God no!" Aaron says quickly as he pushes past me into the house.

"Come in," I say belatedly, shutting the door. "Something I can do for you?"

"Yeah, you can get dressed while I go in the kitchen and make a pot of coffee."

"I'm not getting dressed, I am going back to sleep."

"No, you're not and if you don't get dressed, you're going to look pretty silly walking into headquarters in those shorts, your wrists cuffed behind your back."

He sounds serious. He even looks serious. I decide to get dressed.

A few minutes later I walk into the kitchen. The coffee is made and Aaron has rustled up some raisin toast and butter.

"What? No eggs?" I say.

"I didn't want to appear pushy," he says. "Sit down."

I sit.

"You're being awfully official this morning."

"That's because this isn't a social call."

"I gathered that," I say slathering butter on a piece of toast.

"Tell me about Avery Sterling," Aaron says.

"What about him?"

"What's your relationship?"

"Don't have one. Why? What's he saying?"

"Not a lot. He's dead."

I stop slathering, Since Aaron is a higher up in the Homicide Division at Parker Center, it is unlikely Sterling died of the chicken pox. His presence here in my kitchen at this hour is also disquieting. I decide to lay out my position right away in no uncertain terms.

"I swear to God, Aaron, I didn't do it," I say emphatically.

"I'm sure you didn't, Joe, although there will be those who disagree with me. For example Detective Vito Ciello who caught the squeal and is the lead on the case. From what I hear, he is tough, tenacious, and has no use for Hollywood types, especially successful ones like yourself."

"Okay," I say, pouring myself a cup of coffee and resuming my slathering, "tell me about it."

Aaron fills me in. A friend on night shift called him with a heads up, knowing that Aaron and I were friends. Sterling was found by the janitor around two a.m. lying in a pool of blood on his office floor. He'd been shot twice, once in the head and once in his private parts. Whoever did this was one angry hombre. The medical examiner put the time of death around half past midnight, give or take thirty minutes, and subject to verification from the autopsy report. The employees were immediately checked out and all three verified that I had been one of the last four people to see him alive. The other three, of course, were the employees. One man, a film editor, said he witnessed a violent argument between Sterling and me. I was seen leaving the premises but could easily have returned later in the evening unobserved.

"And maybe the janitor killed him because he didn't like the size of his Christmas bonus. Come on, Aaron, that's a lot of ifs and maybes that don't mean a damned thing and incidentally, we had a confrontation that was not violent, not even close."

"You don't have to sell me, Joe. I'm on your side. But just for the record, where were you around midnight this morning?" Aaron asks.

I give this considerable thought before I reply.

"You're not going to like this answer, Aaron. Neither will your Detective Ciello."

"Try me."

"I was up on Mulholland Drive with a flat tire and no jack and if it weren't for a really considerate Hispanic gentleman in a pickup truck I'd still be there."

"And the time frame for this inconvenience?"

"Between eleven-thirty and one a.m."

"What about this truck driver? He have a name?"

"Pedro."

"Pedro what?"

"Don't know."

"How about a plate number for the pickup."

I shake my head.

"Sorry, didn't know I'd need it. But I can tell you that Pedro is married, lives in Pacoima and has three daughters."

"Fascinating."

"I told you you wouldn't like it."

"I don't mind it," Aaron says, "but Detective Ciello is going to hate it."

"Probably so."

Aaron gets up and brushes away some crumbs from his suit.

"I think at the moment he's still interviewing the employees and supervising the crime scene but sometime today he's going to get around to you. Be warned."

He starts for the front door and I follow him.

"Thanks for coming by," I say.

"What are friends for, Joe?" he says with a smile, opening the front door. "But just remember, this isn't my case and I can't walk all over it, even if I think Ciello's acting like a jerk."

"I understand," I say.

He claps me on the shoulder and gives me a little squeeze and then he goes down my walkway toward his car which is parked at curbside. I watch him drive away and then I go back inside.

I'm really not hungry but I finish off the toast and coffee and then hop in my car and drive to the office. I arrive at eight o'clock beating my secretary Glenda Mae by a whole six minutes. When she sees me already at my desk reading the morning paper, she is depressed beyond words. The hour between eight and nine is "her time" and I am only in the way. I am not sure what she actually does with this hour but I suspect that it has something to do with letter writing and phone calls to old friends, most of them still back in Mississippi. Glenda Mae is the brightest woman I know but for reasons known only to her, she is content to avoid the competitive rat race and settles for making her boss look good in the eyes of the world. Besides brains she is also possessed of a movie star beauty having been Homecoming Queen at Ole Miss two years in a row and first runner up to Miss Mississippi in the Miss America Pageant. She no longer cites the year of this achievement but it makes no difference. Over the years she hasn't lost a brain cell or gained a wrinkle.

"Oh, my God," she says in a near-shriek, "what are YOU doing here?" As if I were a long-lost first husband here to fight about alimony payments.

"Sorry. I lost my head," I say. "Just ignore me."

"How can I ignore you?" she sputters, "when you'll be—-you'll be sitting there!"

I feel guiltier than a three-year old with a mouthful of verboten jellybeans.

"But I have no place else to go," I whine.

"That's not my fault," she says as her level of annoyance rises.

"Close the door. You'll never know I'm here."

"I'll know," she says fixing me with a beady stare.

"Try anyway," I say, "and I promise I won't say a word to you until nine o'clock."

She hesitates, then says, "You'd better not." She turns and leaves my office closing the door firmly. Some might call it a slam. I don't. I am a wimp.

I reach for the container of coffee I brought in with me from the deli. It's empty. The coffee maker is outside in the anteroom next to Glenda Mae's desk. Now it's a pretty good chance she's out there making the morning pot, lacing the ground coffee with a generous helping of chickory as she always does. But maybe not. Maybe she doesn't get around to the coffee until 8:30 or even quarter to nine. I consider going out there to look but that has dangerous implications. I promised 'not a word'. I think I'd better stick to it. Sullenly I pick up my paper and leaf through to the entertainment pages looking for Phineas Ogilvy's daily column reporting on the heroes and villains of the day and other gossip only barely fit to print. My eye falls on my coffee container. I squirm uncomfortably, then pick it up and throw it in my wastebasket. I try to read, still thinking about a fresh cup of coffee. I'm starting to obsess and hate myself for doing so. Who's the boss in this relationship, anyway? And of course, I know the answer to that one and at nine o'clock and not a minute later, I'm going to march out to Glenda Mae's desk and demand my morning cup of joe. Actually, I won't have to because at this exact moment, Glenda Mae enters carrying my steaming mug of coffee which she silently places on my desk and then turns and starts out.

"Thank you," I say.

She whirls around and waggles a finger at me.

"Not a word," she says and goes out.

I smile. She's priceless. I don't know what I'd do without her.

I turn my attention back to the paper and for the first time I notice the photo of Louis B. Mayer framed in black. The old lion died eight days ago. Two days later a funeral service was held at the Wilshire Boulevard Temple. Five thousand people attended, over half of them forced to remain outside. Anyone who was anyone was there. Actors, producers, directors, politicians, statesmen, clergymen, they came from all parts of the world to pay their respects. Jeanette MacDonald sang "Sweet Mystery of Life". Spencer Tracy spoke the eulogy. Today Phineas has written his own eulogy to the old warhorse. Mayer was loved and he was hated. Samuel Goldwyn said the huge turnout was due to the need of many to see with their own eyes that Mayer was really dead but Goldwyn's attitude was in the minority and Phineas wrote as much. No matter what you may have thought of the man personally, he and a handful of others embodied what was known as old Hollywood, the traditional Hollywood that thrived through a devastating depression and an agonizing world war, creating entertainment and escapism for a nation that had had more than it's share of reality. I did not know Mayer well, not as well as Phineas, but the little I did know, I liked the man. He was strong and he fought hard for the values of family entertainment. If he insisted on creating idealized portraits of Americana, so what? It was no sin and the studio's box office receipts proved that the country agreed with him. I finish the article, proud of my friend who for one day has left his acerbic sense of humor on the shelf.

The intercom on my phone buzzes. I pick up.

"Nine o'clock," Glenda Mae says cheerily. I glance at my watch. So it is,

"Thanks for the coffee," I tell her.

"My pleasure. So, what can I do for you, boss?"

"How about getting me Jill?"

"Consider it done," she says, disconnecting.

A minute later she gives me a double-buzz on the intercom and I push the lit up Line One button on the phone.

"Good morning, beautiful,"I say.

"Thank you, sir, but I'd be seeing to new glasses if I were you."

It's not Jill at all but the wise and ancient Bridget O'Shaugnessy, Jill's cook and housekeeper and governess all rolled into one. She says 'sore' for 'sir' and her brogue is thicker than eight-day-old stew.

"And a fine good morning to you, Bridget. Where's the lady of the house."

"Asleep, sir. Herself had a bad night."

I don't like the sound of that. Jill's been having too many bad nights lately. Her doctor's diagnosed her with chronic anemia and whatever she's taking for it knocks her out. I don't think the guy's a quack but I do think she needs another opinion. While Jill and I are no longer romantically entangled and haven't been for five years, she's the mother of my daughter and I care about her.

"And before you ask, sir, Julio has already taken the little one to her kindergarten class."

The 'little one' is my daughter Yvette who thinks I am her Uncle Joe but it's okay because she loves me like a father. Julio is the gardener who doubles as a chauffeur and who also doubles as the family bodyguard. An ex-Marine, he packs a chrome-finish .45 automatic which he knows how to use. Over the past several months Jill has become increasingly paranoid about Yvette's safety as well as her own. Julio gives her peace of mind. He's expensive but she can afford him. A successful career as an authoress of children's books has made her rich.

"Did she say anything about tonight?" I ask.

Friday is our weekly family supper at Biff's All American Diner, but this Friday I have to attend a fundraiser being thrown by Danny Thomas and so the switch to Wednesday. We also plan to take in a showing of Disney's new movie, 'Old Yeller'.

"She said not a word, sir, but I'll bring it to her attention the moment she awakens."

"Thanks, Bridget," I say and hang up. I hope nothing fouls up the plans for tonight. Yvette's looking forward to it and as for Jill, she's lost too much weight and her skin has that indoorsy pallor. She's been house-bound far too long and I'm going to make sure she starts getting out more.

I hit the intercom button.

"Yowzah," Glenda Mae says.

"Yowzah yourself, gorgeous. Do we have a number for Joe Cotten?"

"If we don't, I'm sure Bertha does."

"Orson Welles is staying at his house. Get him for me, please."

"I'm on it."

A couple of minutes later she's back.

"Mr. Welles is out for the day. He'll be back by six o'clock and the lady of the house is on the line. She wants to invite you for dinner."

I pick up and Lenore Cotten and I gab for a couple of minutes. I graciously decline her invitation and she understands why. She promises to have Orson call the minute he shows up. I thank her and hang up. I think Avery Sterling's demise is something Bertha needs to know about so I head down the hallway to her office.

She is surprised but not shocked.

"I knew that weasel was bad news. He had that look in his eyes. You didn't kill him, did you, Joe?"

"Nope."

"Are they going to arrest you for it?"

"They might."

She shakes her head.

"How is it you keep getting mixed up with dead people?" she asks.

"I don't work at it."

"Maybe something in your disposition."

"Maybe so."

"I'm having lunch with Steven McQueen. Want to join us?"

"Who the hell is Steven McQueen?"

"Obviously you didn't see The Defenders the other night?"

I snap my fingers regretfully.

"Darn. I missed it."

"He's the hot new boy toy. Bob Stevens just signed him to star in a pot boiler based on a Harold Robbins novel."

"Exciting," I say, unmoved by this recommendation.

"Hilly Elkins is going after him and that's good enough for me," Bertha says.

"Ah, a war between the women. Always intriguing."

"Scoff if you like, Joe, but one day you'll be glad we've got him."

"If we get him."

"We'll get him," she says, her eyes narrowing into little slits of determination. I love it when she gets like this. She has the fighting spirit of Knute Rockne and twice the smarts. I'm sure glad she's on my side.

I head for the door, wishing her good luck. I've decided not to waste the day waiting for Detective Vito Ciello to come to me. I shall beard the lion at the crime scene and get this nonsense over with. I never get that far. I duck my head into my office to tell Glenda Mae where I'm going and the first thing I notice is this water buffalo sitting on one of our expensive leather sofas. He regards me curiously and then gets to his feet. I see no sign of Glenda Mae. Either she's on a bathroom break or she's tied up in the coat closet.

"You Bernardi?" he asks.

"That depends. Are you armed and dangerous?" I ask.

"Huh?" he says as he peeks inside his jacket at some sort of weaponry. Good guess on my part.

I ignore his rejoinder to my question,

"I'm Joe Bernardi. How can I help you?"

"My employer would like to speak to you," the buffalo says.

"I'm available," I say. "Who's your boss?"

"Good. We will go see him."

"I'd just as soon talk here," I say. "Who's your boss?" I repeat more firmly.

"My car is downstairs," he says moving to the door,

"Wait a second, bozo. I want to know who you are and who you work for or we're not going anywhere."

He hesitates, then opens his jacket wide so I can see the pistol he carries in a shoulder holster.

"I'll drive," he says.

"Good idea," I say. "You drive."

CHAPTER FIVE

Far from being threatening, the big guy turns out to be something of a doofus. His name is Oscar Trippi and years ago he was a professional wrestler who fought under the name Oscar the Ogre. His most famous match, he was quick to tell me, was fought against Gorgeous George at Madison Square Garden in 1949. He even managed to pin Georgie before the ref got into things and threw the match George's way. George was a flamboyant personality who relied on his showmanship and not his wrestling skills to make a go of it. Before every match he would climb into the ring and spray himself with expensive French perfume. "Sissy boy," Oscar had told me. "He smelled like a flower shop. I gave him no respect. The referee beat me. Not George." I think Oscar will hang onto that moment until the day he dies.

We're heading west on Sunset Boulevard with Oscar at the wheel of a new Cadillac El Dorado which is not owned by Oscar but by his employer who I have learned is Jacob Silverstein aka Jake Silver, well known TV spieler for cheap jewelry. Oscar proves to be as garrulous as he is beefy and he assures me that he is eternally grateful to Mr. Silverstein for giving him the opportunity to serve. A true gentleman, Oscar says. Kindly and considerate, not like that son of his. He blesses himself as he says Avery's name but makes no move to retract the sentiment.

"You didn't like him", I say.

"He broke the old man's heart."

"That seems to have bothered you a lot," I say.

He looks at me quickly with a scowl but doesn't respond and then turns his attention back to the road. We pass the Riviera Country Club on our left and by now it's obvious we're heading for the Palisades. On several occasions Oscar swerves slightly left of the traffic line and at other times he edges over onto the shoulder of the road. This is when I first notice the black-rimmed eyeglasses jutting from his jacket pocket. For a moment I am tempted to suggest he put them on but since we are having such a lively and informative conversation, I decide against it.

"I assume that Avery wasn't a particularly likable person," I say to Oscar, tossing out a chunk of bait, "but it's hard to imagine anyone wishing to actually kill him."

He turns and looks at me, bug-eyed with disbelief.

"You think that?" he sputters as the car lurches to the left

"Watch the road!" I scream, my entire body stiffening up in abject terror.

He gets us back on track.

"Wait until you meet Pauline. Then we'll see what you think," he says.

"Pauline? Who's Pauline?"

"The grabber. You know what I mean, money grabber? She was using him but the kid was smarter than that. She got screwed good while she was getting screwed good, you know what I mean?" He grins and laughs at his little joke. I get it.

"And those other ones, the ones who worked for him. Feh!" He spits without benefit of saliva to make his point.

"And what's the matter with them?"

"Takers. You ask around, you'll see. "

He slows and takes a turn into the Highlands area. No getting around it, this is one of the nicer areas in Greater L.A. Close to the ocean, cooled by sea breezes, far from the congestion and polluted air of downtown, this is home to the famous and not so famous, the wealthy and a lot of average Joes who got in before prices started to skyrocket. We make another turn onto a street lined with gracious two story houses. An old man is walking out to get his morning paper which has been tossed onto his driveway. I do a double take as I recognize Francis X. Bushman, a silent movie idol who earned his stardom playing Messala in the 1925 version of "Ben Hur" which William Wyler is in the process of remaking with Chuck Heston as Ben-Hur. Word is either Stephen Boyd or Richard Egan is in line for Bushman's role. I wonder if Wyler will be able to find a small part for the old timer in this new version. It would certainly be a nice touch.

"So, Oscar, tell me more about Pauline," I say.

"There's nothing to say. She sells herself cheap."

"Hooker?"

"No. Nothing like that. For her husband. She fucked the kid to help her husband. He never knew."

"What's that supposed to mean?"I ask.

He glances in my direction.

"You ask a lot of questions," he says.

He turns the wheel and we pull into the driveway of an imposing two story Spanish stucco with a ceramic tile roof. The lawn is lush and green, the flower bed meticulously cared for and in full bloom. A Mexican gardener is trimming the hedge on the edge of the property. I am impressed.

"He is waiting for us around back," Oscar says as he leads me along a slate path that girds the house. The rear of the premises is just as impressive as the front, dominated by an Olympic sized pool which is lined by small cabanas for changing. Seated at a wrought iron table on the nearby terrace is the familiar figure of Jake Silver.

He seems smaller and thinner than he does on television. He has deep set brown eyes and his thick head of hair is silvery grey. He is wearing a silk bathrobe and navy blue pajamas. Sitting across from him is a young man in a grey cotton sweat suit. They are in the middle of breakfast. Oscar leads me to the table.

Silver looks up at me and half-smiles.

"Thank you, Oscar. You may go now."

"Yes, Mr. Silver," Oscar says and he trundles off into the house.

Silver continues to appraise me and then he says, "Thank you for coming, Mr. Bernardi. May I offer you some breakfast?"

"Thanks, no. I've eaten."

"Then please sit and join us for coffee. "

He gestures to the man across from him.

"My associate, Mr. Webster."

"How do you do?" I say.

Webster manages a nod. He, too, gives me a long once over as I sit down. Silver takes a fresh cup and pours coffee into it. He hands it to me. I thank him. So far this is all very cordial and polite. I wonder when the hammer is going to fall, whatever hammer that may be.

"My condolences on your loss, sir," I say.

"Thank you."

I might as well have said this is a lovely pattern on your chinaware for all the impact my sentiment might have had on him. His eyes roam around the yard settling on the pool.

"That's where he died, you know."

"Excuse me," I say, confused.

"James Whale. The previous owner. That's where he died. Some say accident. Some say suicide. I lean toward the latter. I think the old queen just got tired of living."

Whale, a flamboyant homosexual, is something of a film legend having directed 'Frankenstein' as well as 'The Invisible Man' and numerous other movies in all genres. He died earlier this year and apparently Silver wasted no time getting his hands on this property.

"The police were here early this morning. They woke me from a sound sleep." He pauses thoughtfully. "I suppose I am sorry my son is dead," Silver says, "although he gave me nothing but grief his entire life. During his formative years I was not an attentive father and he never let me forget it. To compensate I gave him whatever he wanted no matter how absurd. His so-called motion picture company is a perfect example of Avrom's disconnect with reality. Did you kill him, Mr. Bernardi?"

The question comes out of the blue and I am startled by it. I think I stammer before I reply. "No, I did not, sir."

"I understand you threatened him."

"No, I did not."

"I am misinformed then."

"We had words. It was not a threat."

"Perhaps not. We shall see. You were in business with my son."

"No."

"Something to do with Mr. Welles."

"No."

"Come, come, Mr. Bernardi. I can't be misinformed about everything."

I take five minutes to explain to Jake Silver the circumstances that involved both Orson and myself in Avery Sterling's life. He listens intently and then nods.

"I am anxious to talk to Mr. Welles but I can't seem to locate him. Mr. Webster has checked all the major hotels and he is not registered."

I glance over at Webster who is giving me a hard look.

"Where can I find him?" Webster says.

"I have no idea," I say. "And if you think that Orson Welles had anything to do with your son's death, you are totally misguided."

"Perhaps," Silver says, "but one way or the other I will locate him and I will talk with him."

His voice is cold and matter-of-fact as it has been ever since I arrived. I've seen more grief expressed by a six-year old over a dead turtle than I have by Jake Silver over the loss of his only son. He looks at me and it's as if he has read my mind.

"I am not a man given to displaying emotion, Mr. Bernardi, so forgive me if I forego the tears. As I said earlier Avrom and I were never close personally but there are two things that I can't let go of. Good or bad, he was my son, and secondly no human being deserves to be shot down like a dog. So believe me when I say that I will learn who killed him and Mr. Webster will see to dispensing justice on Avrom's behalf."

"Something, I presume, that doesn't involve the police."

"That is correct. The California court system is a playground for unprincipled lawyers but in this instance their participation will not be needed. When you told me that you had nothing to do with my son's death, I hope you were telling me the truth, Mr. Bernardi. Until the guilty party's identity is revealed, everyone will be equally suspect in Mr. Webster's eyes. Do I make myself clear?"

"Very much so," I say as I stand, "and I hope your executioner here gets it right because if he comes after me, I intend to blow his fucking head off. Now get Oscar out here. I need a ride back to my office."

At that moment I look to my left as a woman appears in the open doorway that leads into the veranda. She's blonde and buxom but this morning she has given up the mink coat in favor of a silk bathrobe over a diaphanous nightgown. In the sunlight she also seems a good deal older than she did charging out of that elevator into Avery Sterling's offices. Our eyes lock for a moment and I can see that she recognizes me but then she turns away and goes to the sideboard to pour herself a cup of coffee.

"Good morning, Henny," Silver says cordially.

She chooses not to answer him preferring to inspect the breakfast array.

"Yes, good morning. Nice to see you again," I say, unwilling to let her avoid me.

"You two know each other?" Silver asks.

"Certainly not," the woman known as Henny says quickly and I spot a barely perceptible look in her eyes, a slight shake of the head and I realize she is imploring me not to pursue this.

"No, my mistake," I say. "Sorry."

I get my ride back to the city but not with Oscar. This time my chauffeur is Webster, first name Douglas. He is as clam-like as Oscar was loquacious. He's a good looking young man, almost John Derek handsome, but there is something in his eyes and in the quirky way he smiles that sets my nerves atingle with dread. One would think that Oscar would be Silver's enforcer but there's a gentleness about Oscar that this predator doesn't possess. My guess is, he's an amoral man who has pledged blind fidelity to Jake Silver. It is a lethal combination which he proves when he pulls up in front of our office building to let me out. As I reach for the door handle, I feel his steel grip on my left arm.

"One more time, Bernardi, just so we understand each other. As a favor to Mr. Silver, I am going to deal harshly with the person that killed his son. Whether that person is you or if it is Mr. Welles, I don't really care. If it's you I will shoot your nuts off, stuff them into your mouth and then blow your head off. Mr. Welles can expect the same. Do I make myself clear?"

"Perfectly," I say. "But what makes you think it was me or Orson Welles that popped Junior. Why not one of those guys in the office or maybe even Pauline."

"Pauline?" For one brief moment he almost smiles. "The Princess wouldn't know which end of the gun the bullets came out of."

"But maybe her husband does."

Webster shakes his head.

"A whole lot of people had a whole lot of reasons for keeping the kid alive. Two didn't. You and the fat man."

"How about—-?"

"How about you stop asking so many questions, Bernardi. Your ass is on the line here but to prove that I am a reasonable man I will give you until noon Saturday to produce Mr. Welles. Otherwise—" He leaves it unsaid but his meaning is clear.

He releases his grip and I push open the door and climb out of the car onto the relative safety of the sidewalk. As I watch Webster pull away into traffic, I pray for the protective arms of the police.

CHAPTER SIX

I don't wait long.

I have been back at the office for a total of twenty-six minutes, dashing off a thank you letter to Ava Gardner who has sent Yvette a stuffed kangaroo from her location shoot in Melbourne, Australia. She's there filming 'On The Beach' with Greg Peck. I'm not sure if Kazoo, the Roo, is going to excite a five-year old but I could be wrong. I suspect my difficulty in fathoming the workings of the female mind may also include kindergartners as well as octogenarians.

My intercom buzzes.

"A gentleman from the police here to see you, Mr. Bernardi," Glenda Mae tells me in her most professional voice.

"Have him come in," I respond in kind.

A moment later the door opens and a slim dark-haired man in a brown suede sports jacket and tan flannel slacks enters. His white shirt is unbuttoned at the neck and his green and gold striped tie is yanked down a couple of inches. Aside from a police special in a shoulder holster this is the best indicator of copdom I know of. He smiles as he approaches my desk and flashes the tin. I already know who he is but I wait for him to confirm it.

"Detective Vito Ciello, Mr. Bernardi. Placere di conoscerla."

"Sorry but I don't speak the language," I say.

"But you are Italian?"

"On my father's side. I'm told my mother was Albanian."

"Good combination. May I sit?"

"Please do, Officer."

"That's Detective."

"Detective," I say.

He sits, looking around at my plush digs in the process.

"Nice. Very nice," he says appreciatively. "I love the movies. I go at least twice a week, sometimes more."

"Our industry could use a lot more like you, Detective," I say pleasantly.

"Oh, I'm pretty sure you do all right, Mr. Bernardi. At seventy-five cents a ticket how could you not?"

He smiles back at me but there's no humor in his expression. Aaron was right about this guy. He reeks of success envy.

"You know why I'm here," he says.

"Sure."

"Tell me about last night."

"What do you want to know?" I ask.

"Everything," he says.

So I tell him everything from beginning to end. My visit to Sterling's office at four o'clock to view the cut of 'Touch of Evil'. My acrimonious departure around six-fifteen, my chance meeting with Orson Welles in the Scandia bar, dinner with Bertha and Tony Randall and finally, my departure for home interrupted by a flat tire.

"So you left the restaurant about ten minutes to eleven, is that right?"

"More or less."

"And when did you go to Sterling's office?"

"I didn't."

"Didn't you? You leave for home, maybe a forty five minute drive, you pull into your driveway at one-thirty. Either you drive very very slowly or you stopped at some babe's house for a quickie or, and this is the one I like, still fuming over your fight with Sterling earlier in the day you return to his offices to have it out with the arrogant little prick."

"I told you I had a flat tire."

"So you called Triple A."

"No, I was nowhere near a phone."

"I see. Then you changed the tire yourself."

"No. I had a spare but I'd left my jack in my garage."

"Really?" he says with an arched eyebrow.

"Really", I say, as I reveal my good fortune with Pedro.

"Pedro from Pacoima."

"That's right."

"With a wife and two daughters."

"Yes."

"But no last name."

"None he told me."

"And no plate number for the truck."

"He had one. I don't know what it is. I really didn't look."

"This wetback, did he speak English?"

I glare at him.

"You're a bigoted son of a bitch, aren't you, Detective?"

He shrugs. "Not really. Just wondering if it would do any good to run an ad in the Valley News. Pedro, please call cops. Movie mogul needs your help."

"I know you're being facetious but I'll run the ad for a month if you think it will help."

Ciello nods. "And if for one minute I believed your story, I'd tell you to do it."

"It's the truth," I say. "Dammit, Detective, this is ridiculous. I hardly knew the man. I met with him twice. We had a disagreement over a business matter and he started screaming invective at me. I responded in kind and that's all there was to it. I yelled at him. Angry people yell. It doesn't mean I killed him."

"Hold that thought. We'll get back to it. Now, where can I find Orson Welles?"

"What for?"

"I want to question him."

I'm ready to throw up my hands. "You can't seriously believe he had anything to do with Avery Sterling's death."

"Why? Because he's a big movie star? On the contrary, Bernardi, I find that in this town, the bigger you are, the more privileged you think you are."

"Oh, please," I say in total disgust.

"Fatty Arbuckle," he says.

"You have got to be kidding."

"1921. He rapes Virginia Rappe, killing her in the process but no jury was willing to convict him of anything. He's a celebrity. He's America's Funnyman but a lot of people weren't laughing. Maybe your fat guy thinks he has the same kind of immunity."

"You're out of your mind," I say.

"Am I? A couple of weeks ago outside of The Friars Club, Welles is waiting for his car. Sterling engages him in conversation. A minute or so later they're raising their voices. Sterling tries to grab Welles' arm. Welles shoves him away and says, "Stay away from me, young man. I know how to deal with people like you."

"He was angry. He raised his voice. That's not a threat."

"The parking valet thought it was. Where is he, Mr. Bernardi?"

"I have no idea." Not a lie. Lenore Cotten didn't know where he was either.

"He didn't tell you where he was staying?"

"No, he didn't." Not a lie. He's not the one who told me.

"And you haven't talked to him today?"

"No, I haven't." Again, no lie.

"If you're covering for him—"

"I'm not."

Ciello mulls that over and then abruptly stands.

"I want you at Metro tomorrow morning, Mr. Bernardi. Eleven o'clock. Don't be late."

"What for?"

"I'll need your statement." He goes to the door and opens it.

"I just gave you one."

"I want another one with my partner present as well as a police stenographer. And I'll need your fingerprints as well."

"And will I be under arrest?"

"Not yet."

"That's comforting. Look, Detective, I have a busy day tomorrow."

"I'm sure you do," Ciello says, "but I can come get you with a warrant if need be. Your choice. Just let me know." And with that, he gives me his crooked little smile and leaves.

I lean back in my chair. This day is not going well. It's obvious Ciello wants to toss me in the slammer, me or Orson Welles, and I don't think he's too particular which of us it is. And meanwhile Jack Silver has made it clear he plans to eviscerate his son's killer and I have the distinct feeling I am near the top of his list of candidates for the procedure. Of course I could always follow Ciello's lead and lay the whole thing on Orson Welles. But that doesn't seem very sporting and besides he didn't do it. I'm almost positive of that. Its clear that I need help and I need it fast. I call my friend Aaron Kleinschmidt at Parker Center.

"I told you, Joe, I can't interfere. This is Ciello's case."

"I've been threatened by a cold blooded son of a bitch named Webster and Ciello doesn't seem to give a damn. I guess he figures if I end up dead, he can close the book on the case."

"Don't dramatize."

"I'm telling you, Aaron, this guy Ciello is a brain dead jerk."

"And don't exaggerate."

"I'm dead serious. Silver had me kidnapped from my office and driven to his house at the Palisades and for a while there, I wasn't sure I was going to get out alive."

"Don't waste my time on this, Joe," Aaron warns.

"I'm not. Webster implied that if I didn't produce Orson Welles by noon Saturday he would kill me."

"Then produce him."

"He might kill Welles."

After a pause, Aaron says with a sigh, "Okay, I'll check these people out on the q.t. I don't need you dead."

"I know," I say. "The paperwork."

"Damned right. I'll get back to you. But Joe, remember, this isn't my case and I am not going to step on Ciello's toes. Not for any reason."

And he hangs up.

Now I'm puzzled. Not for any reason. This doesn't sound like Aaron. There's something else in play here that I'm not aware of and whatever it is, it's obvious Aaron's not going to tell me about it.

I buzz Glenda Mae and ask her to try Lou Cioffi for me. Lou's the ace crime reporter for the *L.A. Times* and a good friend. Maybe he can give me some insight into Vito Ciello that Aaron can't or won't. When she comes back on the line she tells me Lou is out of the office so she left word to call me back. I ask her to try Orson again and again we strike out. He hasn't returned to the Cotten house. Again she leaves word, both office number and home phone.

I check my watch, then pick up the phone and call Jill. She picks up after the first ring

"Sorry I missed you earlier. I slept in," she says

"Good for you. I think you need the rest. What does Doctor

Quackenbush say?"

"He's not a quack and he's upping my medicine."

"And does he have the vaguest idea what's wrong with you?"

"Absolutely. Mild anemia complicated by chronic insomnia brought on by overwork."

"You haven't worked much in weeks," I say.

"I'm just telling you what he told me."

"How about tonight?"

'Fine, but without me."'

"Aw, Jill—"

"You said it yourself. I haven't done much work lately. I want to sketch out some ideas for a new character."

"It'll keep. You need to get out."

"No, Joe, you take Yvette. You'll have a good time and she's dying to see this movie."

"If you're sure—"

"I'm sure," she says.

Which is how I end up In Biff's All American Diner with my daughter, me with a bacon cheeseburger and Yvette with her usual "paghetti". She tells me two jokes she heard in kindergarten. They are pointless and unfunny but I laugh nevertheless and we chat a lot about school and new friends and her drawings. After supper we walk a block to the theater on the corner for the 6:30 showing of Disney's "Old Yeller".

I don't know exactly when the evening turned to crap. Maybe it was when the rabid wolf went after the calf or when Old Yeller fought the wolf but got bitten in the process and contracted the rabies or maybe it was right after the kid Travis shot and killed Old Yeller to save his friend Arliss. I don't really know. All I know is,Yvette is sitting next to me bawling like a hungry six-month old while I am wiping my watery eyes, a condition caused by a child-hood allergy. I think back to the ferocious whale in "Pinocchio" and the evil queen in 'Snow White" and I wonder what it is in kindly old Walt Disney that makes him want to cause children to cry their eyes out.

I get Yvette home by nine o'clock but her tear stained face does nothing to endear me to Jill who is waiting at the door. Yvette is reliving the dog's tragic death while I shrug my shoulders in a helpless apology. Jill manages a smile, blows me a kiss and waves goodbye. I get going while the going is good.

I'm pulling into my driveway when I hear the phone ring in the kitchen. I hop out from behind the wheel and hurry to the side door that opens into the kitchen. I grab at the receiver and hope I've caught the call in time.

"This is Joe," I say somewhat breathlessly.

"Joe. Orson here."

Thank God, I think to myself.

"Orson, thanks for getting back to me. We have a glitch on this Avery Sterling death that you ought to know about."

I quickly recount my morning meeting with Jake Silver and his two cronies, emphasizing that Silver wishes to meet with him and that Silver is a man to be taken seriously. I then tell him that Detective Vito Ciello is likewise anxious for a face to face and he, too, is a man not to be taken lightly. I also explain that Ciello harbors the notion that he, Orson, is at the moment a viable suspect in Sterling's murder.

"Nonsense," Orson says.

"I agree," I say, "but just to ease my mind, do you have an alibi for Tuesday evening, say from eleven o'clock until one a. m.?"

He says he does and I am relieved.

"Tell me about this half-witted public servant," Orson says.

I describe Ciello as accurately as I can including his total lack of awe for motion picture stars. I mention Ciello's Fatty Arbuckle analogy. Orson laughs out loud and then there is silence. For a fleeting moment, I'm afraid he might have hung up.

"Orson?"

"Thinking, Joe. What time did you say you were meeting with this detective?"

"Eleven o'clock. The squad room at Central Division."

"As I recall you are good friends with Phineas Ogilvy who writes the movie column for the *L.A. Times*."

"I am," I reply.

"Do you suppose that you could persuade him to just drop by Central early tomorrow morning?"

"I might. What did you have in mind?"

"An accidental meeting. I explain to Phineas that a wild-eyed police detective out to make a name for himself is considering charging me with the murder of a young producer which is ludicrous because the young man has been trying to help me in my problems with Universal which is recutting my new picture 'A Touch of Evil' despite my strenuous objections even to the point of letting knowledgable industry professionals view my first cut which they have found to be first rate without need of alteration and—." He pauses. "Well, you see where I'm going with this, don't you, Joe?"

"I do, Orson, and you are a sly fox."

"So I have been told and if Ogilvy is the crusader against studio bullying that I remember him to be, this tragedy might turn out to be a boon to my unfairly maligned motion picture."

Indeed, it might, and I tell him so and before we hang up we arrange to meet at Central Division shortly before eleven. Orson and I will meet with Ciello jointly and if Phineas accepts my invitation to join us, it should turn into an intriguing couple of hours.

The next morning, I arrive at the office early and at 8:59, I hesitate outside my office. When my minute hand hits 9:00 I open the door a crack and peer into my anteroom. Glenda Mae is sitting at her desk. She looks up.

"Okay?" I ask hopefully. I want no repeat of the other day.

She smiles and crooks her finger, beckoning me in.

"Thanks, boss," I say to her as I enter.

"Think nothing of it," she replies.

"I need coffee and then about an hour of peace and quiet to do some heavy thinking so hold my calls. If anyone needs me, I'm not available. If it is urgent I have left town. If it is a matter of life and death, I passed away earlier this morning and services will be held tomorrow afternoon at Forest Lawn."

She laughs as she always does when I get downright goofy. I start for my office door when the phone rings. She picks up. I scowl at her in warning waggling my finger.

"Mr. Bernardi's office.....I'm sorry, Mr. Bernardi isn't in yet. May I take a message?...'"

Glenda Mae's face screws up into a mask of anger.

"I beg your pardon, ma'am, I am not a goddamned liar..... Is that right?.... Just a moment." She puts my caller on hold. "The bitch says it's a matter of life and death. Shall I invite her to the funeral?"

"Did you get her name?" I ask.

"Henrietta Hanks," Glenda Mae replies.

I hesitate for a moment, then take the phone.

"This is Joe Bernardi," I say into the receiver. "I just walked in the door."

"And this is Henny Hanks," she says. "We need to talk."

"I'm tied up. Call me tomorrow."

"I know who killed Avery," she says.

"Good," I say. "Tell the police."

"The last time I talked to a cop, he was putting me in cuffs and I was kicking him in the shins."

"All right, then. Tomorrow morning—"

"Screw tomorrow morning," she says. "You know that little coffee shop up the block from your building. I'm sitting in a back booth. I'll see you here in ten minutes." With that she hangs up.

She's drinking coffee and smoking a cigarette when I slip into the booth opposite her. From the looks of her ashtray she's been here a while. She's also gone to some trouble to hide her identity. A hat that completely hides her blonde hair and dark glasses with red frames that conceal her eyes. She has a bruise on her chin and when she takes off the glasses one of her eyes is puffy and it's not from tears.

"Thanks for not ratting me out back at the house," she says. "Not that it did much good. Jake caught on we had some connection and he punched me around for a while."

"Sorry," I say.

She shrugs. "What's to be sorry about? I'm an ex-hooker. It comes with the territory. But I never told him anything."

"Good for you, but I'm still sorry."

The waitress comes to the table. I order coffee. It doesn't excite her but she smiles and walks off.

"You said you knew who killed Avery," I remind her.

"Yeah. I know. And I'm telling you so that you can tell the cops."

"Why would I do that?"

"Because if you don't, in a few days you're going to be resting your tuckus on a marble slab in the morgue."

"And you don't tell them yourself because—-?" I pause, awaiting her answer.

"I told you, I don't talk to cops. Besides, if Jake finds out it was me who blabbed, I'm the one sleeping on marble."

"Okay, so who was it?"

"Douglas," she says.

"Douglas Webster?"

"That's right."

"Why?

"The money, that's why. In his will Jake leaves 5% to me and 5%

to Douglas and the rest would have gone to Avery except where he's gone, he won't be spending any inheritance."

I shrug. "It only makes sense that Silver would leave the bulk of his estate to his son."

"So is Douglas."

"What?" I say, not sure I heard right.

"Douglas is also his son. The mother was a hat check girl in a speakeasy run by Capone. For years Jake paid the bills, even put the kid through college. When he graduated, Douglas came to Jake and asked for a job. He knew all about what happened and told Jake so. Jake gave him a job at one of his San Diego stores and sales tripled in a year. Jake brought him to L.A. where he's been ever since,"

"And Jake is so grateful to this bastard kid of his that he cuts him 5% in his will."

"Nice, huh? Doug's loyal, works hard, does everything right. That little shit, Avery, mooches every buck he can from Jake and Jake can't hand it over fast enough. This dumb movie company is burning money and the kid has no idea where it's going and meantime Doug is watching as Jake's estate starts to shrink like a guy's johnson in an ice cold shower"

"So Douglas kills Avery to stop the drain which is good for you since you also get 5%." I look her in the eye,

She knows what I'm driving at. "Forget 5%. Doug has proof that he is also Jake's son and with Avery dead, when Jake dies, he's going to go for all of it."

"Makes sense," I say. "Do you have any proof?"

"Proof is for cops," she says.

"Then your accusation is only theory."

"Yeah, and I also have a theory that the Mojave Desert is mostly sand." She slides out of the booth and looks down at me. "You tell the cops what I told you, they'll get their proof, believe me."

She walks off as the waitress comes to the table and leaves my coffee and the check. I'm in no mood for the coffee. I scope out the check. Forty cents. Two cups of joe. Us working stiffs have to take care of other working stiffs. I leave three bucks on the table and at last, head for the police station.

CHAPTER SEVEN

True to his word, Orson arrives at Central Division at exactly 10:55. He is only a minute behind me. We have both been beaten here by Phineas whose distinctive metallic gold Lincoln sits in a parking spot a few yards away from where I have parked my Bentley which I am unwisely continuing to drive, even though I still haven't replaced the ruined tire or remembered to put the jack back in the boot. Caution to the winds, I say. Others might say, "Idiot!"

"Have you explained to Mr. Ogilvy the nature of our problem?" Orson asks as we head for the entrance.

"Not in detail. The broad strokes, yes. Since the interview is with you, I thought it best for you to describe the situation in your own inimitable fashion."

Orson smiles broadly.

"And you were right to do so, Joe. I shall dazzle him with my account of my dilemma, skewering the dolts at Universal-International in the process. It will make for fascinating reading."

I nod. "Be careful with Phineas, you might get some dazzlement thrown right back at you."

Phineas rises from the visitor's bench and approaches us, exuding a smile. He is a big man in the sense that Orson is also a big man, heavy around the waist, hulking shoulders, and a little jowly in the face. When they approach each other I am afraid they are going to collide like two bull whales about to fight over a sexy cow but, no, they stop short of that and shake hands warmly. Like Orson, Phineas is a raging heterosexual although he gives the appearance of being otherwise. He is also flamboyant and loves to draw attention to himself, again a trait he shares with Orson. And finally both men are Mensa-level brilliant but where Orson chooses to use his mental capacities to write and direct works that may alter and perhaps improve the world, Phineas prefers to sling arrows at the efforts of second-raters from the safety and comfort of his plush office at the *L.A. Times*. As best I can recall, Orson has never been on the receiving end of one of Phineas's barbed shafts but there is always a first time. I pray this isn't it.

"Bon jour, mon ami." Orson says to Phineas pleasantly.

"Y tu tambien, amigo," Phineas says to Orson, equally so.

"Schon dich kernen zu lernen," Orson says.

Phineas smiles.

"Dank je wel", he replies.

Orson frowns.

"German?"

"Dutch," Phineas tells him.

Now Orson smiles.

"Ahsante sana," he says.

Phineas looks puzzled.

"Portuguese?"

"Swahili," Orson replies.

Before my two companions get a chance to unzip their flies and compare organs. Ciello comes down the stairs from the second floor squad room. He glowers at us.

"You I expected, Mr. Bernardi. You I am happy to see, Mr. Welles." He looks at Phineas. "As for you, three's a crowd."

"Phineas Ogilvy, *Los Angles Times*," he says introducing himself.

"Where's Lou Cioffi?" Ciello asks.

As the lead reporter in the *Times* crime section, Cioffi is well known, and mostly liked, by the cops in the LAPD.

"He wasn't asked to be here this morning. I was."

"Well, I have no time for you, Mr. Ogilvy."

"I didn't expect you would, Detective Ciello, but any time a low level functionary of the city police department has the temerity to insinuate that a major star in the motion picture industry is possibly a murderer, that is news of the highest order and while I don't expect you to talk to me directly, I will have no trouble gathering the facts from these two gentlemen after you have finished interrogating them. Oh, and while I have you, could you confirm the spelling of your last name and may I also have your badge number?"

Ciello stares at him slack-jawed and then finally says, "Get out of my headquarters, you arrogant bastard."

"Delighted to cooperate, sir. And thank you so much for just supplying me with a marvelous title for my column." He turns to Orson and me. "Gentlemen, I shall see you in the parking lot." And with that, he goes out. Ciello stares after him in disbelief.

"Lou Cioffi actually works with that guy?" he says.

"I'm afraid so, Detective," I say.

"Hard to believe. Well, let's go upstairs. You, too, Mr. Welles."

We trudge up to the squad room where we spend the next two hours. He asks me the same questions he asked me yesterday but this time in the presence of a police stenographer and his partner Duffy Jenks, a skinny little guy with tobacco stained teeth and fingers. Jenks doesn't say much but he creates a lot of smoke with a foul smelling little three inch raggedy looking cigarillo. It doesn't bother me but Orson glares at him and when that has no effect, Orson takes out a dark brown cigar that is at least eight inches long. He smiles as he holds it up for Jenks to see and then lights up.

What had been a light haze has now become a thick and noxious vapor, the sort of smoke the Cheyennes used to communicate with the Arapaho when they wiped out Custer.

Finally finished with me, Ciello turns his attention to Orson who does indeed have an alibi. He returned to the Cotten house shortly before eleven o'clock and found both Joe and Lenore still up playing backgammon. Orson joined in, enjoyed a couple of brandies and everyone turned in around one o'clock.

This seems to satisfy Ciello, but before he lets us go, he announces that he is going to take our fingerprints. Orson glares at him.

"I think not," he says. "I have been forthcoming with you, Detective, but I draw the line at ink-stained fingertips. You are acting beyond your authority and unless you are prepared to arrest me here and now, I will take my leave." He stands, still nursing his cigar.

"I can always get a warrant," Ciello says.

"I have no doubt that you can find a brain dead judge in this city of mediocre governance. Please do so. If you need me, Mr. Bernardi knows where to find me," Orson says as he heads for the staircase.

Ciello glares and then turns to me.

"What about you?" he asks.

I point to Orson's retreating figure.

"I'm with him," I say as I follow Orson out.

A short time later the three of us are sitting in a booth at Art's Deli. Orson and I have filled in Phineas on all the pertinent details of his relationship with Avery Sterling, the ill-advised attempt by Universal-International to recut Orson's picture, the surviving first cut which I have seen and pronounced brilliant. Sterling comes across as a pushy no-talent pipsqueak deep into his father's pockets. Phineas is excited. As fodder for one of his columns this is a natural. It contains murder, celebrity, double-dealing by a major studio and an overreaching cop who resents the wealthy, the powerful and the privileged and lets it color his professional judgement.

Phineas has four pages of notes and he chortles as he goes over each one. "This is excellent," he says. "I cannot wait to write this. The absolution of an industry giant, the revelation of a biased and self-serving policeman. All the elements. I shall accept my Pulitzer with great humility."

Orson and I can't help but laugh.

"I admire a man who sets his sights on the highest star, Phineas," Orson says. "I just hope this piece has the desired effect of calling off Ciello. I pray it doesn't work in reverse and make him mad enough to come after me with a vengeance."

"What are you worried about, Orson? You have an alibi," I say.

"I certainly do. Of a sort."

"What do you mean, of a sort?"

"It means, Joe, that I didn't actually return to the Cotten home at eleven o'clock. It was more like midnight."

"So, where were you between eleven and midnight?"

"Venice."

"And what were you doing in Venice?" I ask.

"Repaying a loan to a very generous local who, during the filming, was kind enough to lend me a hundred dollars one evening when I had walked out of my hotel room without my wallet."

"I see no problem with that," Phineas says.

"The gentleman was not at home."

"I see. Then someone else—"

"There was no someone else," Orson says. "When the gentleman didn't answer my knock I got back in my car and drove away, seeing no one."

"No one?" I ask.

"No one," he reiterates.

I look at Phineas. Although I'm sure it's true, Orson's story sounds as fishy as my flat tire.

"And then when I arrived back at Joe and Lenore's, the house was dark," Orson continues. "They were in bed and there was no backgammon game so I went in the kitchen and fixed a sandwich and finally retired without disturbing them. But in broad strokes, I think my alibi is still valid."

Phineas and I share a dubious look.

"Perhaps Detective Ciello won't bother to interview the Cottens," Orson suggests.

"Perhaps not," I echo.

All three of us know that he will.

And he does,

The following day is Friday and early in the morning, two things happen. First, I retrieve my copy of the *Times* from my front stoop and with a strong cup of coffee at my elbow, I read Phineas's column. It is entertaining and brilliantly written. It excoriates Universal Studios for daring to meddle with the work of an acknowledged master of the motion picture. In addition it paints a picture of Detective Sergeant Vito Ciello as a mean spirited, biased incompetent with all the investigative skills of a traffic cop. To consider for even a fleeting moment that Orson Welles could be guilty of murder is not only unthinkable, it is buffoonery. The second thing that happens this morning is a phone call that comes into my office at precisely 9:17. The caller is Vito Ciello.

"Okay," Ciello growls, "where is he?"

"Where is who?"

"Don't give me that. Welles, that's who."

"I told you, he's staying at Joseph Cotten's house."

"Not any more, he's not. He packed his bags and slinked away before daybreak. Where is he?"

"I have no idea."

"That story of his, it was bullshit."

"Really? Hard to believe."

"Not by me. Where have you got him stashed?"

"I haven't."

"How about your pal, the queer with the poison pen?"

"Phineas is not queer, Detective, and I can't believe he knows any more about Welles' whereabouts than I do."

"I'll tell you what I can't believe. I can't believe that a swell guy like Lou Cioffi hangs around with that pompous gasbag."

"Freedom of the press, Detective. Live with it."

"Listen, Bernardi, I'll tell you this once and that's all. If you're lying to me, if you're hiding this guy somewhere, I am going to cuff you and toss you in a cell and throw away the key. Do you get me?"

"I get you."

"Meanwhile, just so you know, you're at the top of my list and one way or another, you're going down for this. Get me?"

"Ciello, did anybody ever tell you that you talk just like a cop in a B movie?"

He doesn't answer. I hear a click. He's hung up.

For several moments i stare at my dead phone and then I remember something. I buzz Glenda Mae.

"Do I call your lawyer?" she asks helpfully.

"Not yet. Check LAX, see if there was a flight out early this morning for the Bahamas. If so, connect me to the head of Operations."

A few minutes later I'm taking to Elsie Crabtree, a veteran of TWA who is in no mood to be cooperative.

"Impossible, sir. I am not authorized to reveal the names of passengers on our flights, past, present or future. To access said information you will need a court order presented in person to our Senior Vice President in charge of International Flight Operations at our headquarters in Kansas City."

"So says your corporate manual?"

"Sir, do not josh with me," she says. "I have no sense of humor."

This I had already figured out.

"Look,Elsie, I don't want to be a hardnose about this and I

certainly don't want to jeopardize your job, but if you cannot or will not give me the information I need, then I must respectfully ask you to put me through to Howard. Tell him Joe Bernardi is calling. He knows me. We worked on several pictures together."

This is a baldfaced lie. Howard Hughes doesn't know me from his trash collector. But Elsie doesn't know this and unless she has more brass than Sousa's marching band, she is going to crumble.

There is dead silence on the other end of the line. Then she speaks.

"You are referring to Mr. Howard Hughes?" she asks.

"I am."

"The rumors flying about the company indicate that the board of directors will be terminating Mr. Hughes contract in a matter or days."

Now I am momentarily silent. But I am not so easily quieted.

"A very narrow window but still large enough to replace you with someone more attuned to meeting the needs of the flying public. Never mind, Elsie. I have no time for this runaround and I still have Howard's private number. I'll be sure to let him know all about your lack of cooperation and maybe the next manager will hire you back."

"Five-four-nine," she says.

"What?" I say.

"Mr. Welles is on our flight five-four-nine which left for Miami at 7:10 this morning. He has a connecting ticket via Delta to Nassau International Airport."

"Thank you," I say. "You've been most helpful."

"That's what we're here for," she says, biting off each word as if it were a jalapeno chili pepper. There is a resounding click as she hangs up.

I stare at the phone. This is a depressing development. Ciello wants desperately to reinterrogate Orson. Jake Silver and his minions are likewise determined to grill him like a Kansas City steak. And without Orson around to share the heat, I have a feeling that a target has suddenly been painted on my back. The only question is, who gets to me first?

Glenda Mae appears in my doorway holding an envelope which she waggles at me with a smile. "Special delivery by messenger. It might be a dinner invitation from some hot redhead but I suspect not." She brings it to me unopened and sashays out of the office.

The beautifully engraved envelope bears Lenore Cotten's initials but Glenda Mae was right. Inside is a hastily scrawled note from Orson.

> Joe, dear friend:
>
> Apologies for leaving you to deal with the dead Mr. Sterllng on your own but Noel has a magnificent property which requires a magnificent director. Best of all he has financing. I shall be thinking of you often the next few weeks. Persevere and prevail, my friend, for both our sakes.
>
> Orson

I stare at the letter even more intently than I had stared at the phone. My worst fears have been realized and worse, one of my cherished idols has deserted me in my time of need. Optimistically, I tell myself that things can't get worse although with my luck I'm probably wrong about that.

Meanwhile I have got to do something about my precarious situation and I don't care one whit about Aaron's reluctance to get involved with another cop's case. I need help.

CHAPTER EIGHT

I'm sitting in a booth at the rear of Tony Cavaretta's Trattoria Capri, nursing a beer and nibbling on bruschetta. It's 7:15 and Aaron is late. Either that or he's lost although I doubt that. Tony's place is a well-known hangout for elderly undesirables of Italian heritage, mostly relocated from points east like New York and Miami and Jersey City. They claim to be retired but most cops suspect they still have their hand in their usual activities on a part time basis. The noise level is high and the crowded room reeks of cigar smoke. There is nothing to recommend this dump except the food but that's enough because it is well known that Tony C. serves up the best lasagna west of the Rockies. Dinner on my dime is the price I have to pay for Aaron's help and eating here at this mob heaven is all his idea.

I look up and see him coming through the door, a manila envelope in his hand. Maybe it's my imagination but for a moment I sense the noise level diminishing as the patrons recognize Aaron for what he is, a homicide dick with the LAPD. Then he sees me and strides toward my booth. He stops twice to say hello to a couple of the patrons. The fat guy in the plaid sport jacket I recognize from television. Joey Blue-Eyes Romano has a yellow sheet so long the cops arrest him out of habit. At the next table is a slick guy in a silk suit and a hundred dollar haircut. I don't know who he is but he has the smile of a barracuda and twice as many teeth. Aaron leans in very close to the guy and whispers something in his ear. Whatever it was, it was not welcome. The noise level resumes as Aaron slides into the booth opposite me, laying the envelope on the table.

"Joey Blue Eyes?" I say. "An old fraternity brother?"

Aaron grins.

"Joey and I go back many years to when I wasn't the most upstanding cop on the force. Today, let's say he is an occasional source of valuable information."

"He's your squeal?" I say in disbelief.

"Joey is a believer in free enterprise, Joe. The numbers, prostitution, even protection, but he draws the line at murder. Thinks it gives him and his buddies a bad name."

"Just another public spirited citizen," I say. "Who knew? And the other guy, the one who looks like Eduardo Cianelli on a bad day?"

"Marco Conti. A big time lawyer for the Gambino family back in New York. He's in town to muscle some of the studios into rewriting contracts for a couple of the unions. Six days ago one of my associates in Vice gave him a week to leave town. I was merely reminding him to make his plane reservation early in the morning."

"Or what? The guys in Vice are going to beat the crap out of him?"

Aaron hesitates for a moment, a sly smile on his lips.

"No, the guys in Vice don't do things halfway, " Aaron says.

"You're kidding," I say.

"Do you remember the Hat Squad, Joe, or were you still overseas fighting the krauts?"

"I kind of remember," I say, trying to dredge it up. "An elite unit working directly for the Chief. Anti-mob, something like that?"

"Exactly like that. These goombahs from back East hit L.A. trying to horn in on the locals. They got one warning. Go home. If they ignored the warning, they never saw home again."

"You're saying that—?

"You know what I'm saying, Joe. Either Mr. Conti gets the message or he gets the message."

I can only stare at him.

"And you condone this?" I ask.

"Of course not," Aaron says. "I'm a homicide detective." He looks past me and waves. "Paulie!" A moment later Aaron's favorite waiter comes by to take our order. Lasagna for two, garlic toast and a nice bottle of chianti.

"So," Aaron says as Paulie walks off, "let me tell you about the mess you've gotten yourself into. It's all in the envelope which I got from Ciello's partner, Duffy Jenks."

"I met him."

"Duffy aspires to someday become a gold shield which he'll never be working with Ciello so he's making a friend of me. The envelope is yours to take, Joe. Everything's in there except the police report which you don't need unless you are investigating the crime— which you are not doing." He bites off these last five words emphatically while staring me down.

"I get the message," I say.

"Okay," he says. "So let me give you the big picture. You're right to be worried about Jake Silver. He is a very bad apple. He was born in 1901 and grew up on New York's Lower East Side. By age 10 he was running errands for the gangs that were terrorizing the neighborhood merchants. When he was 16 he slit another boy's throat for looking crosseyed at his sister. A sharp lawyer for one of the gangs got him off and he was promoted to hit man. Common practice. Even a made guy in fear of his life may not see it coming from a kid who looks like he's still in high school. By the time he's twenty Jake goes into business with a guy name Mike Minucci, stealing cash and jewelry from apartments on the Upper East Side.

A year later he kills Minucci so he can have it all to himself. A sharp lawyer gets him off again and one day he disappears from New York and a month later he's setting up business with a jewelry store in Chicago. He does this with all the jewelry he stole while he was in New York but because he's in a new city, nobody puts it together. Inside of two years he has three more stores operating in and around Chicago. Comes the end of the 20's and for whatever reason, Silver smells trouble with Wall Street and instead of buying, he liquidates everything and moves to L.A. Seven months later the market crashes and while stockbrokers are taking headers out of skyscrapers, Silver is sitting on a mountain of cash. In 1930 he opens his first cut-rate jewelry store in L.A. By 1935 he has nineteen stores up and down the California coast, a new wife and a one year old son. The wife is from the social register and the kid gets treated like the Prince of Wales. After the war the wife realizes there is more to life than country clubs and fancy balls and she decides her son needs more toughening up and a lot less privilege. She tries to take him and move out on Jake. Eleven days later she dies in an unfortunate automobile accident on Laurel Canyon Road, going off the roadway and down hundreds of feet to the rocky canyon below. Friends told investigators that she never drove those mountain roads, the twists and turns scared her to death and the investigators finally concluded that there was a first time for everything. The boy, Avrom, returned to live with his father."

At this moment, Paulie arrives with our dinners and I dig in.

"Nice guy," I say. "Where'd they get all this?"

"Police records from New York and Chicago, magazine articles, a few minutes on the phone with cops back east who knew him when," Aaron says.

"And Douglas Webster?"

"A stone cold son of a bitch who follows Silver's orders without hesitation. There's a rumor he's actually Silver's son by an employee from the Chicago days but there's no proof. He started working for the old man right out of college. The first year he was a clerk. Today he's Silver's right hand man. As for Oscar Trippi—-"

"I know about Oscar. We chatted a lot in the car. He seemed harmless enough."

"Did you know he has a metal plate in his skull?" Aaron asks. I shake my head. "He got into a wrestling match with four guys in a dark alley. Three of them were saved by hospital doctors. The fourth went straight to the morgue. Oscar was in surgery for three hours but they saved his life. Now he's fine except for occasional episodes where he loses touch with reality and goes nuts. Mostly it happens when he gets angry."

"I'll try not to piss him off," I say. "What about this Henrietta Hanks?"

"One time prostitute, graduated to Madame who operated a thriving business from an otherwise respectable office building on Lexington Avenue. Silver started out as a client a couple of years before the crash. She was nineteen years old. Pretty soon it got personal, no cash involved. When Silver moved to the Coast, they lost track. Then a couple of months after his wife died in '46, Silver sees an item in the paper about how Henrietta's been arrested in New York City and looking at thirty years. He sends his lawyer and a suitcase full of cash to New York and inside three weeks the charges are dropped. She flies out here to be with him and she's been here ever since."

"Like a fairy tale except for a non-existent wedding ring," I say. "I may cry. Anything on the three guys at the office?"

"Ciello hasn't gotten that far." His expression turns serious. "Look, Joe, these guys are serious and I sure don't like that threat that Webster threw at you. You could ask for police protection—"

"And we both know what that's worth even if you could arrange it which you probably can't."

"I don't want to bury you, Joe."

"I can defend myself," I say,

"With what? That .25 caliber pea shooter you call a pistol? Get serious. My advice is this, hire yourself a bodyguard. "

"I don't need a keeper," I say.

"Yes, you do," Aaron says, "and I'm telling you to hire one right away. Unless, of course, you're going to produce Welles."

"Can't. He's out of the country."

"Then that settles it. I can recommend a couple of guys."

"Not interested, Aaron. You may have faith in Sergeant Ciello. I don't. I'm going to have to get to the bottom of this myself."

Aaron shakes his head.

"Don't do it, Joe," he warns.

"And if I don't who will?" I say.

I stand and take a twenty out of my wallet and lay it on the table. I pick up the envelope.

"Thanks, Aaron. I appreciate everything, even the advice, but hiding or running is not going to get me out of this mess. I'll see ya."

And I walk out, leaving him there. On the way, I even manage a wink for Joey Blue Eyes.

Once home I get to bed at a decent hour but sleep comes hard, My brain dances with visions of Douglas Webster leering at me and Jake Silver grinning about some private joke to which I do not know the punch line although I suspect it might be me. Oscar is in the ring wearing tights and chasing Gorgeous George from corner to corner never quite catching him and suddenly it isn't George he's chasing, it's me. As for the script reader Ryan Walker, he's sitting at his desk behind a pile of scripts that reaches to the ceiling and chortling to himself as he X's huge passages of dialogue from each misbegotten script when suddenly I sit bolt upright in bed, my eyes wide open. I finally remember where and when I once met Ryan Walker whose name is not Ryan Walker at all.

I really don't expect the Crown Sterling office to be open. For one thing it's Saturday. For another, four days ago the guy who signs the paychecks was bleeding to death on his office floor. And finally it is almost certain that whatever business Avery Sterling was conducting died with him on that fateful Tuesday evening. Still I take the elevator to the third floor. The door opens onto the offices of Crown Sterling Productions and to my astonishment through the glass window I see a gorgeous raven-haired young woman at the reception desk speaking on the phone.

I push my way through the entrance door and approach her desk. At first she registers surprise, then annoyance as she keeps on talking.

"I swear to God, Mamie, I thought the guy had grown an extra set of hands. He's grabbing my ass, reaching under my dress, squeezing my boobs, all at the same time. I shoulda kicked him in the nuts.......Of course I didn't. You think I'm crazy. His brother works in casting at Columbia....Naw, I got nothin'. Not even a meeting. Look, I gotta go. There's a guy standing at my desk and he looks like a bill collector....Yeah, catch you later."

She hangs up the phone and forces a phony smile.

"I'm sorry, sir. The office is closed," she says.

"I know," I say. "I'm the chief suspect. Did you get the part?"

"What?" She looks at me funny, like I'm a nut case.

"I was here Tuesday with Avery. You were on a casting call. Did you get the part?"

"I would have," she says, "but they told me I was too short." Or too tall, or too fat, or too blonde, or too flat-chested. Casting directors have a thousand ways to blow you off besides the truth: Lady, you couldn't act if you were playing yourself.

"What's your name?" I ask.

"Who wants to know?" she says.

I reach in my pocket and take out a business card which I hand to her. She reads it without moving her lips and smiles up at me.

"Melanie McBride, Mr. Bernardi, and I am ever so pleased to meet you." A coy smile. Vivien Leigh by way of Scarlett O'Hara. She extends her hand and I take it, kissing her fingertips. She does a good impression of being impressed.

"And I am delighted to meet you, Miss McBride. Is there something I might have seen you in?"

"I don't think so," she says. "I was a Party Guest With Cigarette in 'Will Success Spoil Rock Hunter' and the Dog Walker on Street in 'Pal Joey'."

I shake my head sadly.

"Missed you," I say with regret.

"Last month I was a featured character in a little theater production on the Strip. 'Hallelujah, Miss Wyoming!' "

"Missed that, too." I say.

"The high point of the performance came when I took my clothes off at the end of Act One."

I'll bet it was, I think.

"Let me know if there's going to be a revival any time soon," I say.

"Oh, I will. Most def."

"Meanwhile, how come you're open this morning? I was sure you'd be closed."

She puts in a pouty face.

"We should be but Mr. Webster called last night and told me to open up at the usual time."

"Did he say why?"

"No, but he said to make sure that Mr. Watson was here." She looks around the otherwise empty room to make sure she can't be overheard and then leaning forward, she says quietly, "He's sitting in his office very quietly and he is very, very nervous. I think they are going to check the books."

"Really!" I say, feigning astonishment.

"And about time, too," she says.

"You mean—-?"

She nods soberly.

"What about Ryan Walker?" I ask.

"What about him," she asks.

"Is he here?"

"What for? He doesn't have anything to do with the money end."

"I need to speak to him. Have you got an address for him?"

She gives me that syrupy smile again.

"Seeing as it's you, Mr. Bernardi, no problem."

She checks her Rolodex and then copies the information on a scratch pad. She tears off the sheet and hands it to me. I check out the address. I know where it is. I thank Melanie. Only too happy to help, she says.

I am almost to the door when it is opens and four men sweep into the room. Three are strangers. The other is Douglas Webster. He stops short when he sees me. He glances at his watch and looks back at me.

"Time's up, Bernardi. Do we have a lunch date with Mr. Welles?" he asks.

I smile in response.

"I'll get back to you on that," I say and scurry out the door. Noon is two hours away and I need a plan. I need one desperately.

CHAPTER NINE

I like to think of Reseda as an ant farm. That really isn't fair but that's how I see this sprawling sea of boxy little houses that have sprung up where once there was nothing but orange groves. The sprawl started in '46 and hasn't stopped since. Row upon row, street upon street, little two bedroom one bath shacks on postage stamp sized lots. The initial price was $9000. Now it's double that. Insanity rules. The older real estate becomes, the more it deteriorates, the more it is worth. Some smart economist from UCLA ought to look into this.

I find Ryan Walker's house with a minimum of trouble. Parked in the driveway is a gleaming 1952 Cadillac Fleetwood, Forest Green with an Ivory top, not a blemish in sight, unsullied in any way as opposed to the man who owns it. Maybe that's why it's in such mint condition, a symbol of better days not that long ago. As for the property, it suffers from neglect. The lawn is patchy brown and green and needs a good mowing. Weeds choke what remains of what might have been a colorful garden. The solitary tree on the property looks to be dying from some disease. It cries out for a mercy killing.

I trudge up the flagstone walk and push the doorbell. I hear nothing from within so I knock loudly. Dead quiet. Perhaps he's not home though with the car in the driveway I doubt it. A movement to my right. A curtain falling back into place. Someone checking to see who's at the door. After a moment, the door opens. Ryan Walker stares out at me over the rims of thick-lensed horn-rimmed glasses. He's wearing a ratty cotton bathrobe and well worn slippers. He needs a shave and his hair looks like a wheat field after a hurricane has plowed through.

"Mr. Bernardi," he says by way of greeting.

"Mr. Walberg," I respond.

He laughs and steps aside.

"Come on in," he says, removing his glasses and slipping them into a pocket of his bathrobe.

I step inside and look around the tiny living room. The first thing I see is the Oscar resting in the center of the mantlepiece. It goes back many years but I remember the film and his award is well deserved. Flanking Oscar, two on each side are framed photos of four extremely attractive women.

"I was just proofing a manuscript," he says, "but I have time for a cup of coffee."

"Sounds good," I say.

He sees me admiring his Oscar.

"My first and only and I win it for a lousy whodunit mystery."

"No, I saw it," I say, "and it wasn't lousy at all. 'At Long Last, Farewell', 1938, I think. I was 18 years old."

Walberg beams. "You have a helluva memory, friend. And thanks for the compliment but it was still junk. Most private eye movies are although I will admit Charlie Cobb, my hero, had a certain breezy charm about him. We did four of them, one a year, and then when the Japs hit Pearl Harbor, I went to war and so did Charlie. Some other guy wrote two more with Charlie playing spy games against Nazis. And that was the end of it."

"Ran out of ideas?"

Walberg shakes his head.

"The guy playing Charlie got drafted and six weeks later got run over by a jeep in basic training. End of actor. End of Charlie. "

"Nothing like a sad Hollywood ending," I say.

"Amen," Walberg says.

"You know I'd love to read the script if you've got a copy laying around somewhere. Or any of your old scripts for that matter, I'm thinking of trying my hand one of these days and who better to learn from than the master."

"Well, I'm afraid you're out of luck, Joe. I'm not much for nostalgia. I write 'em and forget 'em. My only concession to days gone by are old Oscar and the four ladies, loveliest women I ever knew. My ex-wives. Come on, let's get that coffee."

We go into his kitchen. At one of the settings is the manuscript he's been proofing. He takes his glasses from his bathrobe pocket and puts them atop the pile of papers, then bids me sit as he goes to the counter and starts to prepare coffee the old fashioned way, in an aluminum percolator.

"So the other day you recognized me," he says.

"I knew I knew you," I say, "but it didn't really register until last night. Joel Walberg, one of the industry's most talented screenwriters, working as a bottom rung reader for a two-bit phony with delusions of grandeur. I don't have to ask how it happened."

Walberg shrugs.

"The House committee and I didn't hit it off very well. I was too scared to defy them and too proud to cooperate so I kept throwing a lot of 'I don't remembers' at them. In the end they didn't have enough to send me to jail but I was on the blacklist even before I walked out of the hearing room." He hesitates, momentarily staring off into space. "Probably dumb of me. Should have told them what they wanted to hear. What do you think, Joe?"

"It depends."

"You mean, was I a Communist? No, but I went to a helluva lot of meetings. Free food, nice looking babes, and once in a while some speaker would almost make sense. I say almost because what these guys were spewing had nothing to do with the way the Comintern was screwing its own country."

"And Avery? Did he know who you really were?"

Walberg laughs.

"Are you kidding? He'd have fired me in a flash. He was a hundred percent American through and through. Hated Commies, tolerated the mob, and loved Congress, every lowlife son of a bitch from every state in the union. Lucky for me the bimbo didn't know either. She'd have had me drawn and quartered. A real Red baiter, that one." He takes down a couple of mugs from a cabinet and pours out the coffee. "What do you take?"

"A little cream, a little sugar."

"Got milk."

"Not a problem. What bimbo are you talking about?"

"Pauline. Pauline Kreitzmann."

"Oscar mentioned her to me. She was sleeping with Sterling. Something like that."

He takes the milk carton from the refrigerator and sets it down on the table along with a sugar bowl.

"Yeah, something like that," he says.

"Tell me about this hot property he had that he wanted Welles to direct or was that just more bullshit?"

"Oh, the property's real," Walberg says. "I oughta know. I wrote it although the name on the cover page is Harold Dempsey. Harold's my barber."

I nod in understanding.

"It's a love story called 'Bad Times' about two of life's losers caught up in the marathon dance craze of the 1930's. Don't suppose you remember it."

"Read about it," I say. "So you just happen to find this terrific script by Dempsey in your huge pile of submissions and it's so good, even Avery can appreciate it."

"You catch on fast, Joe," Walberg says with a sly grin. "Financing is no problem because the kid's old man is footing the bills. Jamie Kreitzmann is set to direct—."

"Wait a minute," I interrupt. "Who's Jamie Kreitzmann?"

"Pauline's husband. She'd been banging Avery for months, with Jamie's blessing, of course, to make sure that Jamie got a directing gig. That was before Avery thought he had a shot at Orson Welles and started chasing Welles all over the city."

"That couldn't have made Pauline very happy."

"Or Jamie either. He threatened to kill Avery if he didn't get the directing job."

"When was this?" I ask.

"Just last week. They were screaming at each other in Avery's office. I wasn't the only one who overheard it. You could hear their voices all over the office."

"So let me get this straight," I say. "Jamie Kreitzmann sends his wife out to bang Avery Sterling in hopes of getting a directorial assignment on a really first class property and the wife, Pauline, who obviously has no self worth or moral compass, is glad to do this for her slimy self-absorbed husband whose level of moral decency rises no higher than a snake's belly. Am I missing anything?"

"Not that I can notice," Walberg says.

"And so when Sterling double-crosses the two of them by pursuing Orson Welles, they predictably become annoyed."

"Very much so."

"So much so," I suggest, "that perhaps the thought of murder finds its way into their hearts."

"Hard to argue otherwise," Walberg observes.

"And yet both Jake Silver and Detective Ciello are looking at me and Orson Welles as prime suspects for merely raising our voices to the little snot."

"It defies credibility," Walberg says shaking his head in wonderment.

"Somehow I'm missing something here."

"So it seems."

"What about Roy Watson?" I ask.

"What about him?" Walberg asks.

"Melanie McBride led me to believe that there was some hanky-panky going on with the company books."

"Well, I wouldn't know anything about that. My paychecks never bounced."

"You think she was feeding me a lot of hot air?"

"I wouldn't go that far," Walberg says. "Melanie, real name Olive Fassbender, sounds like a brain dead gal from a Georgia peanut farm but she knows the score about this place. Don't sell her short even if she is an actress."

We chat for a while longer over our coffee and Joel Walberg turns out to be excellent company. For a guy who has been scourged by Congress and labeled a pariah, he's surprisingly upbeat. He tells me he is in the middle of writing a stage play for the Shubert Organization. They've even given him an advance, seldom the case in the Broadway scene. We gab about old movies and he's a bigger buff than I am which is saying a lot. He tells me he's a dunce compared to Jamie Kreitzmann who he says has eidetic memory and started going to the movies when sound came in. There is nothing Jamie doesn't know, like Greenstreet's weight when he made 'The Maltese Falcon' or who were the first five choices to play Ashley Wilkes in 'Gone With the Wind' before they finally settled on Leslie Howard.

We talk for a few minutes about Joel's Oscar about which he has mixed feelings. He says his character, Charlie Cobb, eccentric, humorous and free wheeling won the award for him, despite the creaky storyline and the over-the-top plot devices. Unbelievable bullshit was the way he put it. In my opinion he is much too hard on himself.

As I look around the interior of the little house, I realize that things have been tough for him because of the blacklist but he doesn't whine about it. His barber, Harold Dempsey, has become a prolific writer of dime-a-dozen TV westerns although he only gets to keep a third of the money. For this he takes an occasional meeting while Joel does all the work. Joel says he can knock out a 30 minute western in one day. I believe him. I've seen the shows.

After nearly an hour of wonderful conversation and reminiscing about old movies, old time actors and actresses and Old Hollywood the way it used to be, I'm out the door. With great effort I manage to turn my attention back to the murder at hand. I am determined to spend some more time with Melanie McBride who apparently knows all there is to know about everything and everybody. I'm especially anxious to know what, if anything, the audit of the company books turned up. I'm also aware that I have less than one hour to produce Orson Welles or suffer some unspecified indignity at the hands of Douglas Webster. This, too, is going to require my attention.

Once on the road I decide to go to the office even though it's closed for the weekend. I could return to Sterling's offices but I really have no desire to bump into Webster again and I can phone Melanie from the comfort of my desk. It also occurs to me that I haven't heard from Bunny since Monday and this is strange.

Bunny Lesher is the woman I am going to marry. Several years ago we lived together in bliss but then a series of unforeseen circumstances befell us and she turned to alcohol and lost track of who she was. Now she is well on the road to recovery, working at a responsible job at the Joplin, Missouri, Globe and it's just a matter of time before she hands in her resignation and travels west to be with me once again. Only one thing bothers me. We have a firm schedule for phone calls. I call her on Mondays. She calls me on Thursdays. But this past Thursday there was no call nor on Friday either and I'm getting a little concerned. Whether she likes it or not I'm going to have to violate our agreement. I need to know what's going on.

I stop at the deli for a chicken salad sandwich and a hot container of coffee and by twelve-thirty I'm seated behind my desk. I fish around in the center drawer for the card Sterling gave me when we first met and I call the number, hoping they haven't left the premises.

"Avery Sterling Productions," comes her voice.

"Melanie, it's Joe Bernardi."

"Oh, hi," she says brightly.

"The gang still there?" I ask.

"Mostly," she says. "Around 11:30 Mr. Webster got a phone call from Mr. Silver and he had to leave but the auditors are still in with Mr. Watson."

Webster's not there. I don't like the sound of it. It's past noon. Is he preparing to make good on a threat? I try to put it out of my mind.

"How's it going? The audit, I mean."

"I don't think well," she says. "I hear a lot of yelling."

"No," I say, "that doesn't sound good at all. Listen, Melanie, the reason I called, if you're not busy, I'd like to take you out to dinner tonight."

"Really?" A voice saturated in disbelief.

"Absolutely," I say.

"Well, I have a date but I can break it."

"Are you sure?"

"It's not a problem. My boyfriend Melvin wants to take me out for a hamburger and then get into my panties. Can you imagine? For a lousy hamburger."

"I can do better," I say. "Ever been to the Coconut Grove?"

"Oh, my God," she says breathlessly.

"Give me your address and I'll pick you up at seven o'clock."

She relays her particulars and I jot them down. When I hang up I can't help but smile. She's an odd combination of worldly wise and total naivete. I like her. Tonight could be fun even though sex is not on the table.

Next I call Bunny in Joplin. I let her phone ring fifteen times. No answer. She's not there. I hang up and call the newspaper.

"Joplin Globe. May I help you?" comes a female voice.

"Hi, I'm trying to reach Bunny Lesher. She might be working today."

"I haven't seen her," the woman says. "She really doesn't come in weekends."

"I know but could you check for me. It's kind of important."

"Sure. Hang on," she says. I hear a clunk as she lays down the phone. I wait patiently, drumming my fingers on my desk. I really don't expect Bunny to be there. Chances are she's out shopping or gone to a movie. After a couple of minutes the woman returns and picks up the phone.

"She's not here," the woman says.

"Okay. Thanks, anyway," I say.

"Are you the good looking studmuffin in the picture on her desk, the guy from Los Angeles?"

"That's me. I'm Joe."

"I'm Wendy. Your picture's gone, Joe. So's everything else on her desk."

"No. Not possible," I say, suddenly in a panic.

"I'm sorry, Joe. I double checked. Her desk drawers have all been cleaned out. Maybe she moved to some other part of the building. I don't know why but it's possible."

"Can you connect me to the business office?"

"Closed for the weekend," Wendy says,

Of course it is, I say to myself, feeling like a dunce. I thank her and hang up. There's a cold feeling in the pit of my stomach. Bunny's done this before. Suddenly afraid, she runs. I thought she was over that, that she finally trusted me. Maybe not. I lean back in my chair and stare at the ceiling. If only I didn't love her so.

Lost in my thoughts, I almost don't hear it. The whine of the ascending elevator. It stops on this floor. We are the only tenants. The people we do business with know we are closed on weekends. I am suddenly very much afraid. I get up from my desk and cross to my office door which is closed. I open it a crack and look out. The reception area is dark. I saw no reason to turn on the lights. The corridor outside the office is dimly lit. The shadowy figure of a man is standing at the glass doorway to our suite. I left the door locked to make sure I wouldn't be disturbed. Now as I look, the man has taken something out of his pocket and is doing something to the lock. I can feel myself start to sweat and my legs begin to tremble. This visit is not casual and this man is up to no good. Suddenly the supposedly locked door swings inward and the man, still unrecognizable, steps into the waiting room. A thought occurs to me. I'm a dead man.

My Beretta is in the glove box of my Bentley. No help there. I look frantically around my office trying to remember if there is anything here that might possibly double as a weapon. I come up empty. No, wait. I move quickly to my concealed bar which is part of one of my bookcases. I pop it open and, aha, sure enough, in the drawer I find the knife I use for peeling lemons. It's plenty sharp but the blade is only two inches long. Not much against a stone cold killer with a handgun. I cross over to my coat closet and duck inside. That's when I remember that there's a sizable pair of scissors in my desk drawer. Also not much of a weapon although Grace Kelly used them handily in 'Dial M for Murder'. I start out of the closet to go to the desk when I hear movement at my door. Too late. I duck back inside, leaving it ajar just a crack so I can see what's happening. I peer out. It's a man. His back is to me. I don't think it's Webster but that doesn't make me feel any safer. He knows I'm here. Foolishly I left my office lights on. Any minute now he's liable to turn around and look in the closet. If so I will be a Thanksgiving turkey. I decide to bluff it out.

"Don't move! I have a gun!" I say from the relative safety of the closet.

I see the man freeze.

"Mr. Bernardi?" he says.

"Drop your weapon on the floor," I say.

"What weapon? I have no weapon," he says. "And please don't point a gun at me. I abhor firearms."

That stops me in my tracks. What kind of a killer abhors firearms?

"Put your hands up and turn around," I tell him.

Slowly he does as I have ordered and immediately I recognize him.

"Please, Mr. Bernardi, I assure you, I come in peace," says Marco Conti, the slick mob lawyer from New York.

Hesitantly I open the closet door and emerge, my hand tightly gripping the lemon peel knife and holding it out threateningly in front of me. Conti looks at it and smiles.

"May I lower my hands now, Mr. Bernardi? I promise you, I will not pit myself against your formidable weapon."

I look down at the pitiful blade in my hand, embarrassed. Conti lowers his hands.

"What are you doing here? Did Douglas Webster send you?"

"No, he didn't and I have no weapon to drop, Mr. Bernardi. My name is Marco Conti—"

"I know who you are," I say irritably. "Why are you here?"

"As a favor to a friend," he says. "I came to get acquainted."

"By using a pick to force my office lock and to say hello to someone non-existent in a deserted office?"

"I saw the light coming from beneath your office door."

"Liar, liar, pants on fire," I say.

"All right," Conti says, "I was here to check you out and to find out what sort of a mess I've gotten myself into."

"That sounds better," I say, "but I still don't know what you're talking about. Now try to forget you're a lawyer and give it to me straight."

"Very well. A high-up member of the Los Angeles Police Department has prevailed upon another high-up member of the Los Angeles Police Department to issue me a stay of deportment."

"In other words, the vice cops are not going to shoot you on sight, at least not today."

"You could put it that way," Conti says. "In return for this accommodation, I have contacted a person of long standing acquaintance and informed him that you, Mr. Bernardi, are important to my work here in Los Angeles and that I would take it as a deep personal favor if nothing untoward happened to you in the foreseeable future."

Aha, I think, the picture is coming into focus.

"And out of this spirit of friendship, Jake Silver has agreed to call off his dogs, at least for the moment."

"Precisely," Conti says.

"Giving you more time to blackmail, cajole and threaten the studio owners to roll over for a new union contract."

"Crude, but more or less accurate," Conti says. "So I am saving your life while you are saving mine. An excellent arrangement."

"You may think so," I growl. I can't wait to chew off Aaron Kleinschmidt's ear. I know he meant well when he called that Vice cop but I don't like this sleazy goombah thinking he holds my marker.

"And while we are on the subject," Conti says, "I understand that you are very close to Jack Warner."

"That's right," I say, "and if you mention his name one more time in my presence, I am personally going to help the guys in Vice toss you off the roof of the Biltmore Hotel. Jack may be a tough old bird but he loves his company and you don't and bottom line, Conti, you're not fit to clean his ashtrays. Now get the hell out of here."

He glares at me, the veneer falling off like maple leaves in October in New York.

"One word from me to Jake Silver—"

"Yeah, yeah, I know. And minutes after I hit the pavement with a bullet in my brain, Vice will have you with a rope around your neck looking for the nearest tree branch. Out!"

He looks like he wants to say something else but he doesn't and grim faced, he turns on his heel and strides from my office. Only then do I put my formidable lemon peel knife into my pocket.

CHAPTER TEN

I pick up Melanie McBride at her apartment on Montana Avenue in Santa Monica. She has two roommates who are apparently in need of medical help for terminal cases of the giggles. One is named Tiffany, the other Alexandra. They are both actresses and common sense tells me that these are not their real names. Because I am supposedly hot stuff in the movie business, I get their full attention while I wait for Melanie to make her entrance. Predictably neither is currently working in the business. Alexandra waits tables at a diner in West Hollywood. Tiffany answers the phone for an ambulance chasing lawyer in Culver City. Both tell me they are available but neither specifies for what.

When Melanie finally appears she is a vision in green silk. I wonder if this kid can act because she has everything else in spades. Looks, style, youth and an endearing personality. I make a mental note to recommend her for a bit part if the occasion arises. I won't say anything to her and if she gets the part she'll never know I was involved. To do otherwise is to invite every wannabe actress in Hollywood to camp out on my doorstep.

It's a short drive to the Ambassador Hotel where the Grove is located. I continue to live dangerously. I have not repaired my tire and I have forgotten once again to stick the jack in the boot. If I get a flat in the parking lot, it's the valet's problem.

Fritz, the maitre'd for the Grove, has been expecting me and greets me effusively while Melanie stares bug-eyed at everything going on around her. The Everly Brothers are set to perform and they are one of Melanie's 'faves'. I look over at her one more time as Fritz leads us to our ringside table. She's starting to look more and more like Judy Garland in "The Wizard of Oz". I whisper in her ear.

"I probably should have asked you this earlier, but exactly how old are you, Melanie?"

She smiles up at me, her grey-green eyes glistening in the muted light of the nightclub.

"Old enough," she says softly.

Fritz seats us with our oversized menus. I slip him a sawbuck. He retreats gracefully as our waiter approaches. Like Fritz, Angelo has been around the club for years. He wishes me a good evening and I respond in kind. He asks for our drink order. Mine's a dry martini on the rocks. Melanie orders a rum and coca cola with a cherry.

She continues to stare around the room like an orphan in a toy store. She leans forward conspiratorially.

"Over to my left. In the grey suit. Isn't that Tab Hunter?"

I follow her glance.

"Yes, it is."

"I just love Tab Hunter. Who's that guy with him?"

"His roommate."

She frowns, obviously confused.

"With all his money, he has to have a roommate?"

I have this overwhelming desire to dig into her purse and check her driver's license but just then Angelo arrives with our drinks. I raise my glass to her. "Skoal," I say and drink.

She drinks as well and then says, "Mine's cold, too." With that she plucks the cherry from the glass and pops it in her mouth. Now I'm starting to worry that people are staring at us.

"So how did it go at the office today?" I ask.

"Okay," she says.

"I don't suppose they hauled Roy Watson off in handcuffs."

"Nope." She continues looking around the room. I can see I'm going to need to be more direct if I expect to get any useful information from Miss Wide Eyes.

"So did they find any problems with the books?"

"I think so. Oh, there's Sal Mineo. God, is he gorgeous."

"He certainly is."

"Who's that guy with him?"

"I don't know."

"It looks like he has a roommate too."

"Melanie, look at me. I need you to concentrate. I need to know what the auditors found out about the books."

"What for?" she asks.

What for, indeed, I think.

"I might be interested in investing in the company. That way we'd keep the doors open and you'd keep your job."

"Oh, I see," she says. "Well, I didn't hear anything official but what I did hear, it kinda sounded like there was a lot of money missing."

"What do you mean, a lot of money?"

"I think somebody said a hundred thousand dollars."

I try not to gulp. That, indeed, is a lot of money and not an insignificant motive for murder.

"Do you think Avery knew about the missing money?"

"Maybe, " Melanie says. "A couple of weeks ago Mr. Sterling and Mr. Watson had a big fight in Mr. Sterling's office and Fiona—that's his secretary, Fiona—Fiona said they were yelling at each other something awful. She couldn't really hear what it was about but I guess it was the missing money."

"Mr. Sterling must have been plenty mad."

“They both were,” Melanie says. “When Mr. Watson went into his office, he slammed the door. You could hear it everywhere.”

“You think he might have been mad enough to kill somebody?”

“Oh, sure, those last few days, I guess we all were,” she says.

I look at her sharply but before I can speak, Angelo arrives to take our order. I select the coq au vin preceded by a small Greek salad. For a side dish, I choose white asparagus with bernaise sauce. Melanie goes for the salisbury steak with french fries and onion rings and another rum and coke with a cherry.

When Angelo departs I try to refocus her on the office drama.

“Melanie, you said you all were angry with Avery. Does that mean you all had reason to kill him”

“Sure.”

“Including yourself?”

“Why not? I mean, not that I did but believe me I had plenty of reasons. He kept saying he was going to use his contacts to get me a good part in a decent movie but every time I went out on an interview, it was always like these casting guys never heard of me and weren’t expecting me. And all the time that I think Avery is setting things up for me, he’s banging the crap out of me.”

“You were sleeping with him?”

“Sleep? Did I say sleep? I said he was banging the crap out of me. In the office. Always in the office. Mostly after everybody had left for the day.”

“I see.”

“On his desk. On my desk. On the floor. In the stock room.”

“Wow,” I say.

“On the big table in the conference room. In the men’s room. The ladies room.”

“I get it,” I say.

“In the hallway out by the elevator—”

“I said I get it, Melanie. The man was a louse. But you wouldn’t have shot him?"

"Shot him? Oh, God, no. I hate guns. I'm terrified of them. My little brother was almost killed by one when he was six. No, I would have stabbed the bastard in the heart. Or poison maybe. But not a gun." I hear a little catch in her throat and I think I see tiny tears starting to form in the corners of her eyes. "I do everything I can to get a decent part and do I get a part? No, I get a sore butt. That's what I get. A sore butt." She scowls and takes another sip of her rum and coke and now the tears are starting to run down her cheeks.

Just then the lights dim, there's a drum roll and a spot hits the Everly Brothers. They jump right into their new hit record, "Wake Up, Little Susie". I think, wake up, little Melanie.

Forty-five minutes later we're into dessert. I've ordered tiramisu. Melanie's digging into a mud pie. Once again I tell her I feel bad about the way she was treated by Avery Sterling. The business is full of skunks like him. It's a hard lesson but one she had to learn. I opine that she won't make the same mistake again. I also warn her that Detective Ciello may have some tough questions for her in the future.

"What for? I didn't kill him," she says.

"I know," I say, "but the police will be looking closely at everyone in the office. Everyone but Ryan Walker, that is."

"And what's so special about Mr. Snooty Nosed Walker? You think his armpits don't smell?"

Oops. I can't tell her who Ryan Walker really is. Slip of the tongue.

"Well, he's just a hired reader, that's all."

"Yeah? Well, he's also a hell of a yeller. This time Mr. Sterling was in the men's room and Mr. Walker followed him in, waving a script and screaming at him like he'd like to cut his throat. Something about a rewrite that Mr. Sterling ordered and Mr. Walker saying the script didn't need a rewrite and Mr. Sterling yelling back who cares what you think and whoever heard of this bozo Harold Dempsey anyway. Like I said, it was a bad week for everybody."

"But it turned out to be a worse week for Mr. Sterling," I say.

"Oh, yeah. You mean because he's dead," Melanie says, performing sadness for me.

Just then the Grove's orchestra segues from a sentimental ballad into some kind of music I have never heard before. Melanie's eyes light up.

"Hey! Wanna dance?" she asks.

"What is that?" I say.

"Chalypso. You know, American Bandstand."

"American what?"

"Bandstand. Dick Clark. Everybody watches it."

Not me.

"Come on, let's go," she says, starting to get up. I grab her hand to keep her seated.

"I don't do that one," I say.

"You're kidding."

"Nope. I have an old war injury from World War Two."

Happily she doesn't ask what WWII was but instead gives me a sympathetic look.

"Oh, that's really too bad."

"I think we should go," I say.

"Sure," she replies, mildly disappointed that we won't be chalypsoing.

We leave the club and walk over to the valet stand.

"Well, where shall we go?" she asks.

"Your place," I say.

"Oh, we can't do that. I have roommates."

"I know, I met them."

"I mean, we can't do it there, not while they're there watching TV."

"Melanie, I'm taking you home so you can get some sleep."

She looks at me, puzzled.

"Sleep? Don't you want to screw?"

I look over at her, suddenly feeling like a protective big brother. This child has no modesty as well as very little self-worth.

"That is a provocative invitation, but, no, as attractive as you are, Melanie, I don't want to screw."

She frowns again.

"Does that mean you're a—"

"No, it doesn't," I say quickly. "My World War Two injury, remember?"

"Guess you're not getting much, then," she says.

"No, I'm not," I say, hoping that my response will end this topic of conversation.

At that moment my car pulls up. I check the tire and we get in. I'm really hoping for silence on the way to her apartment but I don't get it.

"I hope Mrs. Cacavas is going to be all right," Melanie says out of the blue.

"Who?" I say.

"Mrs. Cacavas. Ralph's mother."

"Ralph who?" I ask.

"Our editor. He ran the projector for you the other day."

I remember him.

"Ralph. Of course. What's the matter with his mother?"

"She had a stroke. Almost two weeks ago. Ralph's trying to get her into a nursing home but it costs a lot of money."

"I imagine so," I say.

"Ralph's been going crazy ever since Mr. Sterling refused to give him the money he owed him."

I look at her sharply.

"Money? What money?" I ask.

"The five thousand dollars."

"What five thousand dollars?"

"For bringing him Mr. Welles' movie."

"Mr. Sterling promised Ralph five thousand dollars if he would bring him that first cut of 'Touch of Evil'?"

I start to ask questions to which I already know the answers.

"But he didn't pay him."

"No."

"Did they have a very loud,very nasty fight about it?"

"They sure did."

"In the office?"

"Yep."

"Where everyone could hear?"

"Yep. Ralph said if Mr. Sterling didn't give him the money he'd promised, he was going to kill him."

Why am I not surprised by this? I look over at Melanie on the odd chance that she's joshing me. No, she's dead serious.

I get her to her door none too quickly for my taste. I know she is disappointed that she's going to miss a tussle in the sheets with Bunny's favorite studmuffin but at 38 I have a decaying body to protect and just thinking about Avery Sterling and Melanie on the conference room table is enough to pull a back muscle. A quick hug and a kiss on the cheek and I'm out of there, headed for home and dreaming about a nice hot tub. Me. Alone. In hot water. So what else is new?

CHAPTER ELEVEN

Early Sunday. Just past nine o'clock. I give him fair warning.

"You got the kid this weekend?" I ask.

"Yes," Aaron says.

"You got plans?"

"We're going to the Rams game."

"Go nowhere until I get there," I say and hang up.

Now I'm in my car about a half-mile from Aaron's house. He and I are going to have it out. If he's lucky he'll get to the game on time with his son, Josh, who is really a great kid, and who is set to graduate from Crespi High School in June. At six-four Josh has a basketball scholarship from Stanford. His 3.9 GPA also didn't hurt.

The kid greets me as I pull up to the curb outside the house. He's shooting hoops into the basket over the garage door. As he always does, he challenges me to a one-on-one. I beg off. Maybe later, I say. I don't need the humiliation. He grins knowingly and tells me his Dad is out on the back porch.

Aaron's drinking coffee and reading the front page of the *Times*. He looks up glowering when I appear.

"And who put a hot poker up your ass this morning?" he growls. His displeasure is all for show. We've been friends now for over eight years which permits us to needle and jab one another at will.

"You did, amigo," I say pouring myself a hot cup of coffee. "Yesterday afternoon I'm at my office and I get a visit from this oily mob mouthpiece from New York."

"Marco Conti."

"Marco Conti, who apparently is keeping me alive because of some deal you worked out with the vice squad."

"I sense a hint of ingratitude in your tone, Joe."

"You're putting me in the mob's hip pocket, Aaron."

"Not the case, my friend. Conti's got a one week reprieve for vouching for you with Jake Silver. Inside that week Ciello's going to find Avery Sterling's murderer."

"Detective Ciello couldn't find his nose if he were staring into a mirror and you know it."

"Calm down, Joe—"

"Captain Alfredo Ciello, a 29-year veteran of the force, posted to Parker Center and serving as a Deputy to Police Chief William Parker. Maybe you never heard of the guy but Lou Cioffi sure did."

"I've heard of him," Aaron says.

"I'll bet you have," I say. "Father?"

"Uncle. His father died in the line of duty when Vito was twelve years old."

"So Uncle Fredo gets the kid into the Academy and makes sure he graduates and then he wangles him a plush assignment as a detective in the Central Division which means my life depends on this moron solving a case that would baffle Sherlock Holmes."

Aaron shakes his head.

"It can't be that tough," he says.

"No?" I tell him about Roy Watson and the missing hundred G's and the shouting match, heard by all and Ryan Walker alias Joel Walberg and the screaming match over a Walberg script that Sterling had ordered rewritten behind his back, and Ralph Cacavas who threatened to kill Sterling because he refused to pay Cacavas money he was owed and needed to save his mother's life. And then there was Melanie McBride who was Sterling's favorite punch and who he had screwed over in more ways than one. And wait, I forgot about Henrietta Hanks who stormed past me heading toward Sterling's office muttering, "I'm going to kill the son of a bitch!" And never mind Oscar Trippi who has a plate in his head and could go off like a Roman Candle at the least provocation.

"And you think Vito is going to maneuver himself through all that?" I ask petulantly.

By now I am leaning across the patio table staring Aaron down.

"I cant fight his rabbi," Aaron says quietly. A rabbi is a mentor, a higher-up who shepherds a newcomer's career. In this case family blood enters into it.

"Will you at least promise to be one of my pallbearers?" I say, not flinching for a moment.

Aaron sighs audibly.

"What do you want me to do?" he asks.

"For starters get me a copy of the police report. I can't save my own ass flying blind."

"Okay, I can do that," Aaron says, "as long as it's absolutely on the q.t. I'm too close to my twenty years to toss away my pension."

"Understood. What about Marco Conti?"

"For now he's keeping Jake Silver and his hatchet man off your back. If you're nowhere at the end of the week, I'll jump in and negotiate a peace."

"I still don't like it."

"Live with it," Aaron says. "I have no legitimate reason to arrest Douglas Webster despite his threats and if I did he'd be out in an hour, more convinced than ever that you're involved in Sterllng's death."

"Okay," I say grudgingly.

"You've got five more days."

"I know, I know. When do I get the report?"

"I'll drop it by your office first thing tomorrow morning."

"Fine."

"You still got that gorgeous looking secretary?"

"She's married."

"Too bad. How about the gal at the reception desk?"

"Greta? Available but much too much for you, old pal."

"I'm divorced, Joe, not dead."

"In that case, good luck. Have fun at the game."

"We intend to."

I head back around the house toward my car. I hear the clank of the basketball against the rim and as I appear to Josh I feign a limp.

"Twisted my ankle on a loose rock," I say to him regretfully.

"Tough luck, Mr. B. " the kid says. "Maybe some other time."

"You bet," I say, thinking it will be a cold day in hell before this lanky hustler gets his claws into me.

I hate Sundays. For a lot of people it's a wonderful day. Church for those who believe. Sun and beaches in the summer months, baseball in the spring and summer, football in the fall. But at heart it's a day to be shared with someone you love and aside from those few Sundays I've been able to spend with Yvette, I've been pretty much alone. By choice. I am waiting patiently for the rebirth of my relationship with Bunny and for the past three years I have been convinced it is just a matter of time. I haven't been celibate but in my own way I have been faithful because I knew that she and I would spend many happy Sundays together in days to come. But that is the future, not now, and this particular Sunday I find unendurable. She has disappeared, I know not where, and I can't shake my deep fear that perhaps this time she is gone for good.

I pull into my driveway in a deep funk and the idea of getting rip roaring drunk suddenly looks very appealing. I enter through the kitchen door which adjoins the driveway. The house is quiet, empty, forbidding. A primeval scream rises to my lips but I stifle it. I open the fridge and take out a Coors. I only have three. Unless I go to the store this won't be much of a jag. I pop open the can and take a deep swallow just as the phone rings.

"Yeah," I grumble into the mouthpiece.

"Yeah? What kind of a greeting is that? I've been calling you all morning. Jesus Christ, Joe, where have you been?"

I don't need a photo ID to know who's on the other end of the line. I worked for Jack Warner for seven years. I still hear his voice in my dreams.

"Sorry, Jack, if I'd known you wanted to talk to me so desperately, I would have spent the morning sitting by the phone." I take a swig of beer and sit down at the kitchen table.

"Don't crack wise with me, Joe. I knew you when."

"And I knew you. The miracle is, we still talk to each other."

There's a pause and then he laughs.

"Damned right," he says.

I'm one of the people in the business who really likes Jack Warner and I'm pretty sure he likes me even though I walked away from a cushy job at his studio three years ago to get in bed with Bertha Bowles. Figuratively speaking, that is.

"Anyway, I called to ask exactly when it was that you went over to the dark side,"Jack says.

"What are you talking about?"

"I was walking out of my favorite tobacco shop early this morning with a pocketful of those damned overpriced Havanas when this guy walks up to me and starts talking about union contracts. I know he's not one of the union guys because he talks in complete sentences. Then I find out that he's a mouthpiece for some guinea mobsters back in New York who are hopeful that I will make a juicy deal with the locals and avoid the hassle of a work stoppage or equipment breakage or all those other things that happen when there's no agreement."

"Okay, Jack, I know the guy—"

"So he tells me—-"

"But it's not what you think."

"No? You're not working under the table for the union guys--"

"No—-!"

"—because this guy is throwing your name around like a beanbag at a kid's playground!" Jack has raised his voice to one decibel short of the speed of sound.

"Jack! Take it easy. Your blood pressure," I say.

"Are you selling me out, Joe? Me, who gave you your big break? Me, who made you what you are?"

"Jack, the guy is bullshitting you! I'm not involved and I don't want to be involved. The man knows a man who knows a man who knows me, it's that simple. Tell him to go fly a kite."

"I told him worse than that."

"Vice is all over him like flies on a cow patty. In five days they're sending him back to Little Italy in one piece or several, his choice."

"Five days? Why not tonight for Christ's sake?"

"It's a long story," I say.

There's a long silence.

"Oh,oh," Jack says. "In deep shit again, Joe? What is it this time?"

"Like I said, Jack, long story. When the smoke clears we'll sit down to lunch and I'll tell you all about it."

"I just bought the rights to 'Damn Yankees'. I'm going to need you next year. You going to be alive?"

"I'll work on it. Meanwhile tell Zanuck and the others I've got nothing to do with this guy."

"I'll tell them," Jack says, "but they may not believe me."

"Not believe Jack Warner? Surely you jest."

He laughs. So do I. In a way I miss the old tyrant. Things were never dull. I promise to stay in touch and hang up.

I sit back in my chair and finish off the beer. I am going to have to do something about Marco Conti.

At that moment, my front doorbell rings. I am astonished. The last person to ring that bell was a girl scout selling cookies and that was back in April. I go to the door and open it. Three guys are standing on my stoop. One is dressed in a sport jacket, white shirt, tie, hair combed neatly, pleasant smile. I have no idea who he is. The other two look like escapees from a prison farm. Their ill-fitting rumpled suits don't fool me. These two are trouble, especially the squat two hundred pounder with the oft-broken nose.

"Mr. Bernardi," the sharp looking one says. "Keith Murdock." He hands me his card. He's a union vice-president. He indicates the other two men. "Tony Isaacs, Teamsters. Boyd Kraft, stagehands. May we come in?"

Tony Isaacs,Teamsters, the guy with the busted beak, is standing with his arms folded in front of him, staring at me grimly like a wolf eyeing a crippled rabbit. Kraft has a toothpick in his mouth which he waggles back and forth as he shifts his feet nervously. He does not make eye contact. I have a picture of me stepping inside with these three guys and getting the shit kicked out of me.

"No," I say. "We'll talk out here."

I close the door behind me. My next door neighbor Chuck Bledsoe is in his driveway washing his car. He's keeping one eye on me and my company. If I am to be assaulted, the police will have a witness.

"We don't need much of your time, Mr. Bernardi," Murdock says politely, "There's a man recently arrived in the city named Marco Conti. I believe you know him."

"We've met."

"He's approached me and the boys here about getting involved in the upcoming negotiations with the studios. I told him we needed no help and that we could take care of ourselves. He tried to persuade us that with the backing of his associates back east, we would get an immediate contract under extraordinarily good terms. I repeated myself which was when he told me that you and he were involved jointly in trying to be of assistance."

"He lied," I say.

"The last thing we need is to have our union infiltrated by a bunch of thugs from back East."

"I just told you, he lied," I say. "You want it in writing? I met him once and that was once too often. He's slick as a snake and a world class liar and I have nothing to do with him. Now, is there anything else I can help you with?"

Murdock gives me the fish eye, looks to his two companions, and then back at me.

"I'd like to believe you, Mr. Bernardi," he says.

"Knock yourself out."

"As for me," Murdock says, "I'm a peaceful man. I always believe a problem can be worked out with words. But I have members who think words are a waste of time, hard heads who love the union and everything it stands for. If they thought for a second that gangsters from the east coast were moving in, they'd start breaking heads and once they start there's no telling what will happen. Do you get my drift?"

"Oh, I get it, all right. Stay away from Marco Conti or risk hospitalization or even worse."

"That's not exactly what I said," Murdock replies.

"No, not exactly, but close enough. Gentlemen, this conversation is over. Now get the hell off my property."

I turn and go back into the house, I don't even look to see if they are leaving but as a precaution I engage the lock before I go back to the kitchen to pop another Coors. I cannot believe how quickly my life has turned to crap. Six days ago I was a reasonably happy and successful publicist. Now I am in danger of being whacked by a stone cold enforcer named Webster for a murder I did not commit. If Webster doesn't get me a bird-brained cop named Ciello is ready to put me away for the rest of my life. Meanwhile my friends and associates in the industry think I have suddenly become a tool of the unions and guys like Keith Murdock think I'm a stealth mobster ready to help the Gambino family take over their union. Worse than that, my beloved Bunny is on the run again. Just when I thought we were going to put our lives back together, she disappears. Is she drinking again? Has she suddenly been gripped by fear? I know there are no good answers to any of my questions and I am desolate. My only consolation is that things can't possibly get worse.

For the second time in three days, I am wrong about that.

CHAPTER TWELVE

Monday morning, I'm up early. How early? I've already brewed the coffee and toasted the raisin bread all the while keeping an eye on the wall clock. When the minute hand clicks to 7:01, I grab the phone and dial Joplin, Missouri. It will be 9:01 there and the business office at the Globe will have been open for the past minute.

"Good morning. This is Trudy. How may I help you?"

Her voice is soft and lilting and already I am feeling good about this phone call.

"Hi, Trudy," I say. "My name is Joe Bernardi and I'm trying to get in touch with Bunny Lesher. She doesn't seem to be answering her home phone."

"Lesher, Lesher," I hear her say quietly. "I think I have something on that. Just a moment. Yes, here it is. Miss Lesher left our employ on Friday."

"I see. And did she leave a forwarding address?"

"Let me see. No, it says forwarding address to come. I think she wasn't quite sure where she was headed."

This is ugly news. I've been down this path before.

"Trudy, I have a problem," I say. "Is there anything in her phone records over the past week or two that might give you some idea who she has talked to? It might help me figure out where she's gone."

"Well, I suppose," Trudy says hesitantly. "I've never been asked that before. Just a moment." For a minute or two there is silence on the phone and then Trudy returns. "Who'd you say this was again?" she asks suspiciously.

I think fast.

"Joseph Bernardi. Bernardi, Gable & Lombard, San Diego, California. We are probating the will of Miss Lesher's recently deceased uncle Abernathy who has left her a substantial sum. Several thousand dollars, in fact. You can understand why it's imperative we locate her."

"Why, yes, I do," Trudy says. "I suppose this will be all right. Our records show two person-to-person calls last week to James Kelso at the Ocala Star-Banner."

"That's Ocala, Florida?"

"Yes, it is."

"I don't suppose you have any idea why she made these calls?"

"Oh, I'd have no way of knowing that, sir. I can tell you that up until six months ago Mr. Kelso was employed here at the Globe as an assistant editor and it's generally believed that he left for Florida for a better position."

"I see. And what can you tell me about this guy Kelso. Young man? Not so young? Married?"

A pause.

"And what's that got to do with Miss Lesher?" Trudy asks. "'What did you say the name of your firm was?"

I hang up. Bunny and a guy named Kelso. My stomach starts to rumble. I know what my next step is but I'm afraid to take it, afraid of what I might find out. I'm disgusted by my cowardice. To hell with it. What is, is. I grab the receiver again and ask for Ocala information.

It takes me fifteen minutes but I finally get through to the right guy. His name is Al Cummings and he's a sports reporter.

"Mid-40's, sandy hair, maybe five-ten. Is that the Jim Kelso you are looking for?" Cummings asks me.

"Yes, that sounds about right," I say. "And you say he's gone?"

"Yeah, it was really strange, Mr. Bernardi. Never saw it coming, not really. Friday afternoon, Jim just scooped up his stuff and quit. Walked out the door and never looked back."

"And he never said where he was going?"

"Nope. Maybe I should have picked up on it. He'd been fighting with the managing editor almost from day one. Oil and water. Two guys that just didn't hit it off."

"You think part of the problem might have been trouble at home? With his wife, I mean,"

"Wife? No, Jim wasn't married. I think he got divorced a few years back. Couldn't swear to it, though."

My gastric condition gets worse. Bunny gone. Kelso gone. Gone to where, nobody knows but it's a buck to a nickel that they're together.

"Jim never said a word to me about a rich maiden aunt, Mr. Bernardi. He's sure gonna be surprised by that six thousand dollars."

"That he will, Mr. Cummings. They'd lost track over the last twenty years."

"You say she was a hundred when she died?"

"A hundred and two and seventeen days," I say.

"Well, if he calls me, I'll let him know you're looking for him. Can you give me your phone number?"

"We're in the book," I tell him as I quickly hang up.

With nothing to do around the house, I decide to go into the office where there is also nothing to do. Unless, of course, the union has set up a picket line outside our building or worse, 86 year old Adolph Zukor, the Chairman of Paramount Pictures, is waiting in my reception room ready to flail me with his walking cane for consorting with the enemy. As I drive over the hill to the L.A. basin, I think more and more about getting on a plane and flying east. I know it doesn't make much sense. There probably isn't much more to learn than I know already but I shiver at the thought of sitting helplessly behind my desk, knowing Bunny is out there and not knowing where she is or what she's doing.

I leave my car in the public parking lot next to our building. The new owner is named Chuy and I have the same deal going I've always had. A primo spot where I won't get dented or dinged and a hand car wash every other day. I pay dearly for this but it's worth it. Despite the aggravation I love my Bentley and I treat it like a pampered pet.

There is no picket line outside the building and Zukor is not waiting in our reception area. However, I do have company. Oscar Trippi, aka The Ogre, smiles and gets to his feet when he sees me, wishing me a happy good morning. I respond in kind and ask him what he's doing here.

"Mr. Silver asked me to watch you," Oscar says.

"What do you mean, watch me?"

"He wants to be sure you don't run away."

"I'm not going to run anywhere," I say.

"No, you're not," Oscar smiles knowingly.

"Oscar, I'm not going to have you following me around wherever I go."

"Mr. Silver says I will."

"And if I have a date with a young lady?"

"I go with you."

"And when I go home at night?"

"I go with you."

"I will talk to Mr. Silver about that. Go sit down."

"I'll wait by your office," Oscar says.

"Out here," I say.

"By your office," he says more forcefully. He starts to open his jacket to display his weapon.

"Don't show me that!" I bark at him. "Follow me."

He tags along as I return to my office where he sits in the small settee opposite Glenda Mae's desk. He settles in. He has no book, no magazine. He just sits as I walk toward my private office door. I hesitate at Glenda Mae's desk.

"Who's your friend?" Glenda Mae asks me quietly.

"My keeper," I say, also quietly

"I thought buffalo were extinct."

"Be charitable, Glenda Mae," I say, "he's actually a pretty nice man."

"What do they feed him? Cows?"

"Next time I hear some producer is looking for a comedy writer, I'm going to recommend you."

"Don't. I'd much rather work for you than make a decent living."

"Ha ha. When you get a chance, put me through to Aaron."

"Can't keep up, eh?" she says with a wink, reaching for the phone.

A minute later Glenda Mae double beeps me and I pick up. Before I can say anything, Aaron tells me, "I've got it." He means the police report.

"Anything interesting in it?" I ask.

"My friend, there's nothing in this report that ISN'T interesting."

"Lunch?" I suggest.

"Anyplace where we won't stumble across a cop. This thing is burning a hole in my pocket. I'd just as soon it didn't burn down my career."

I suggest the Brown Derby on Wilshire. As far as I can recall I've never seen a cop in there, certainly not one in uniform and as for plainclothes, the Derby has an interesting policy. They don't "forget" to give anyone their check, not even the Mayor. For many on the force, this is an affront to their profession. We settle on twelve-thirty and Glenda Mae makes the reservation. Since I have no pressing project at the moment I spend the morning writing letters I've owed for up to a month and making long overdue phone calls. Then, at twenty to twelve, I buzz Glenda Mae.

"Is he still out there?" I ask.

"Uh-huh," she says.

"What's he doing?"

"Sitting quietly. If he doesn't move in the next ten minutes I'm going to water him."

"Get me Bertha," I say.

In a few moments my partner comes on the line.

"What's up?" she asks.

"I need a favor."

"What kind of favor?"

I tell her.

"I can do that," she says.

Ten minutes later I emerge from my office. Oscar gets to his feet. I wave him back down.

"Sit, Oscar, I'm not going anywhere. I have too much work to do." I turn to Glenda Mae. "Have the deli send me up a pastrami on rye and a bag of chips. If my friend is hungry, take his order."

At that moment, Bertha enters, all business as she approaches me in mock annoyance.

"Joe, where the hell is that cost projection for the Jimmy Stewart movie?"

"I'm working on it, Bert," I protest.

"Well, god damn it, Joe. Work harder. Preminger's not going to wait all year."

"Okay," I say.

"Otto wants us bad but he's not going to retain us without looking at the numbers."

"I said okay, Bert," I reply testily, eye to eye with her. "You'll have it by four o'clock."

"Fine," she snaps as she turns to go, then stops short when her gaze falls on Oscar. She looks back at me. "Who's this?" she asks.

"Oscar," I say.

She steps toward him.

"Hello, Oscar, I'm Bertha," she says.

He stands politely and her gaze moves upward as he does so. He's got her by a foot.

"How do you do?" he says.

"Great. Are you an actor, Oscar?"

"No, missus, I am a wrestler."

"Same difference," she says. "Ever do any acting besides faking a broken back? Stage maybe. Commercial for television. Anything like that?"

"Yes, a commercial. Many years ago. For a tire company. Tires were strong, couldn't be hurt, like me, Oscar the Ogre."

She nods and tweaks his bicep appreciatively.

"How would you like to be in a movie, Oscar?"

"I don't know. Maybe."

"My client Gene Fowler is making a picture called 'I Married a Monster from Outer Space' and he needs a big guy just like you. The pay is good. Very good."

"I would have to ask my employer for permission."

"Sure, ask away," Bertha says. "Meanwhile you come on down to my office while I get Gene on the phone. I want him to meet you." She takes him by the arm and starts to lead him toward the door. He looks back at me, conflicted.

"Don't worry about me, Oscar. I'll be in my office working."

That seems to satisfy him because he goes off with Bertha willingly. I wait for a good thirty seconds, then turn to Glenda Mae.

"I'll be at the Derby on Wilshire with Aaron if you need me. Don't tell the big galoot and don't let him look in the office. I'm busy working and can't be disturbed. When I return I'll try to figure out a way to get back behind my desk without him knowing. I may need to pull a gag like this again."

Glenda Mac smiles.

"I'm on it, boss," she says.

CHAPTER THIRTEEN

The Brown Derby is a silly looking restaurant and has been for decades. Its exterior is shaped just like a, well, a brown derby. To understand the Derby is to understand the Los Angeles culture with eateries shaped like hot dogs and mortuaries with drive-up windows so one can view the remains of the deceased and pay final respects without leaving the comfort of one's car. Once you accept the city for what it is, living here is easy. Hollywood, with all of its glitz, is right at home in L.A. and Avery Sterling, a poster boy for chutzpah and wannabe aspirations, was right at home in Hollywood. His killer is most likely a wannabe just like himself and it's going to be up to me to find out who that miscreant is because if I don't I may find myself on Variety's celebrated obituaries page. I fervently hope that my friend Aaron Kleinschmidt is going to help me avoid that fate,

Daisy, the cornfed hostess from Abilene, leads me to a rear booth where Aaron is nursing a ginger ale. He smiles wanly as I sit across from him, ordering a Coors from Daisy in the process. The noise level is considerable and Aaron looks around the large crowded room uncertainly.

"Who are all these people?" he asks me, shaking his head.

I check out the crowd.

"The slick fellas in suits laughing the loudest are movie guys trying to put a deal together which they probably won't do and the quiet ones with the sourpuss faces are out of town tourists wondering where all the celebrities are."

Aaron nods in semi-understanding.

"How's the food?"

"Terrific."

"Can I get a hamburger?"

At this moment Daisy returns with my beer and two menus.

"See for yourself," I tell him.

Daisy leans in close.

"Anything good I should know about, Mr. B.?" she asks.

Daisy is one of the thousands in this city who work to eat and dream of being the next Marilyn Monroe. If I know of a picture that's getting ready to gear up and it might have a bit part she'd be right for, I tell her. Twice it's worked out. That's why she adores me.

"Nothing today, Daisy, but I won't forget you."

"You never do," she smiles. "Bernice will be right with you," she says as she hurries back to her station by the door.

"Two-seventy-five? They gotta be kidding," Aaron says scanning the menu. He looks at me. "Two-seventy-five for a lousy hamburger?"

"It comes with a green salad," I say.

"I don't care if it comes with caviar."

"Don't worry about it. I'm on an expense account."

At that moment, Bernice appears. Aaron grudgingly settles for the hamburger, well done, and ranch on his salad, and I go for the club sandwich on toast. As she walks off, I say, "Okay, show me."

Aaron reaches in his pocket and takes out a folded sheaf of papers.

"You're gonna love this, Joe. I could say that Ciello hasn't a clue and in terms of reasoning out this case, he doesn't, but he does have clues. He has more clues than he knows what to do with."

Aaron hands me the report and I open it up. Three pages. Typographical errors abound and the rules of grammar have been mangled beyond comprehension. Still I silently fight my way through it. A third of the way in I furrow my brow. Further along, deeper furrowing. By the time I'm finished I am speechless with disbelief.

I read aloud. "Deceased shot twice." I look up at Aaron. "He doesn't say where in the room Sterling was shot, where in the room the body was found, what type of wounds, amount of blood at the scene, position of the body, lividity, signs of rigor mortis, if any, upon discovery."

"Check the addenda," Aaron says. I flip to the back page. It's single spaced and addresses most of my questions. "Ciello wrote the report, his partner, Duffy Jenks, added the addenda. Duffy's no dope."

"And Ciello's a moron," I say.

"Only on a good day," Aaron replies, taking the report back from me. "I talked at length with Duffy who gave me the report. Duffy's not flashy and he has no rabbi which is why he has been stuck at Detective One for so long but he knows what he's doing. Anyway, here's where we are. Preliminary time of death as you know was set between midnight and one a.m. Duffy promises to get me a copy when the official autopsy report is issued by the medical examiner. Figure another couple of days because the coroner works on the squeaky wheel premise. If the lead detective isn't screaming at him to hurry up, he doesn't rush it. Ciello has been silent and the M.E. has been taking his time.

"Let me guess," I say. "Ciello's first homicide".

Aaron smiles. "You got it," he says, "and no one including the division commander has the guts to take it away from him." He flips to the back page. "Anyway, continuing from Duffy's addenda, there were two visible bullet wounds. Head and private parts. No gun was found at the scene. Presume that both wounds came from the same gun but we won't know that for sure until we get a ballistics report and we won't get that until the M.E. digs the slugs out during the autopsy which we know he has not yet started. Hell, Joe, we don't even know the caliber."

I am dismayed and show it. Aaron sees my expression.

"I know, I know, but for the moment there's nothing to be done. Now, Joe, take another look at the section dealing with things found at the scene. Page two." He hands me back the report.

I flip back to page two and look over the itemized list. One woman's earring, gold, with single diamond. One pair of men's eyeglasses with black plastic frames. One movie script, written by a guy named Dempsey, apparently tossed against the wall, where it came apart, pages strewn everywhere. One white handkerchief with the initial W carrying traces of blood in the wastebasket. Three petals from a white carnation on the carpet near the door.

"Wow," I say quietly. "Although I suppose it's possible these things were there long before Sterling was killed."

"You think so?" Aaron asks. "Check the fingerprint paragraph,"

I find it and scan it, reading aloud as I do.

"Only two sets of fingerprints were in evidence at the crime scene. One belonged to the victim, the other to a person unknown. A search of the Department's fingerprint files failed to come up with a match." I scratch my head. "That's odd. Only two sets of prints."

"Not odd, my good friend," Aaron says, "Duffy interviewed Building Maintenance. Sterling's suite of offices, which was empty at the time, was thoroughly cleaned between eight and nine o'clock."

"Which means—" I say.

"Which means," Aaron says, "that Sterling returned to his office. The person with the mystery prints showed up as did the person or persons who left behind the earring, the glasses, the script, the bloody handkerchief and the remains of a white carnation."

I have a picture of Henny Hanks charging past me into Sterling's offices wearing gaudy diamond earrings. And Oscar Trippi, driving like a maniac with a pair of black-rimmed glasses peeking out from his jacket pocket. And who owns that bloody handkerchief? Probably Roy Watson, the greedy embezzler, but it could just as easily have been dropped by Douglas Webster. The Dempsey script was undoubtedly tossed against the wall in a fit of rage by Joel Walberg. As for the lady with the white carnation, I haven't a clue.

I put my head in my hands. My brain is reeling. I feel a migraine coming on. I look up at Aaron hopefully.

"I don't suppose Detective Ciello fingerprinted the major suspects in the case for comparison to the prints in the office."

Aaron smiles at me.

"I don't suppose you are absolutely right," he says, "but here's the good news, Joe. When he finally gets around to it, the prints won't be yours."

I give him a sick smile just as Bernice arrives with our lunch. I have totally lost my appetite but not so Aaron who digs into his burger with gusto and pronounces it worth every penny of my money.

I drive back to the office in a state of a befuddlement. I was hoping the police report would have one solid clue that would lead to the identity of the killer. Now I have a half-dozen clues and solid confirmation that the detective leading the investigation is a bona fide idiot. I also don't need a calendar to tell me that I'm running out of time. I've got until Friday to reveal the murderer. That's the day Marco Conti gets shipped back to New York and Jake Silver is free to diddle with me as he will.

I park my car and start toward the front entrance to the Brickhouse Building which houses our tenth floor suite. As I approach an attractive woman in a slinky silk dress wearing sunglasses and a wide brimmed straw hat is eyeing me carefully. As I reach her, she steps in front of me.

"Mr. Bernardi?" she says.

"That's me. How did you know?"

"I was given a description,"she says.

"Oh? Did it say tall, dark, handsome, debonair, terrific smile?"

She doesn't smile at my quick wit.

"No, I was told six foot one, brown hair, brown eyes and paunchy around the middle."

Instinctively I suck up my gut.

"I'm amazed you stopped me with such a misleading description. By the way, you forgot to introduce yourself."

"My name is Pauline Kreitzmann."

"The wife of that not-so-famous director, Jamie Kreitzmann?"

She ignores that.

"We need to talk," she says. "Your office will do fine."

"Afraid not. Oscar the Ogre is sitting patiently in my anteroom waiting for me to appear from my office door. When I come in from the other direction, he is going to be disappointed and probably mad and maybe doubly so when he sees you. He doesn't like you very much, Mrs. Kreitzmann."

"Nor I him, Mr Bernardi. Where do you suggest we go?"

"I know a nice little motel on Sunset Boulevard," I say, "but no, that might lead to complications. How about right here?"

She gestures toward the parking lot.

"How about your car?" she suggests.

"How about right here, Mrs. Kreitzmann," I say sharply, "and make it fast. I still have to deal with Oscar."

She hesitates and looks around, making sure we are not being observed.

"I understand you are working with the police in the matter of Avery Sterling's death," she says.

If she's talking about Aaron Kleinschmidt, in a sense she's right.

I decide to play along.

"And if I am?"

"I know who killed him."

"Really?" I feign interest,

"The dark haired little bitch at the reception desk."

"Melanie McBride?" Now I feign shock.

"That's right. Little Miss Mattressback. She'd been screwing Avery to get ahead and he'd promised her the star part in this new movie he was preparing."

"The Orson Welles project," I say.

She lowers her glasses slightly and glares at me over the top of the frame.

"That's the Jamie Kreitzmann project," she hisses.

I shrug.

"I was misinformed," I say.

"The day before he was killed, Avery contacted Kim Novak's agent to check her availability. That night, after everyone had left, the little tramp cornered Avery in his office and pulled a gun on him. She threatened to kill him if she didn't get the part." I watch as Pauline's eyes morph from cerulean blue to bright green. "Avery was able to wrest the gun away from her and sent her home."

"He didn't fire her?"

"He should have," Pauline says, her eyes turning a deeper green. "The next night she finished the job."

"Avery let her keep the gun?"

"No, he put it in his desk drawer but she knew where it was."

"That's a hell of an accusation, Mrs. Kreitzmann. How do you know all this?"

"Avery told me."

"Then you two were friends."

"Yes."

"Intimate friends?"

"Hey!" she says indignantly. "I'm a married woman."

"And this is Hollywood," I respond.

"Oh, I see," she says. "You believe all that crap about how I was sleeping with Avery to further my husband's career."

"I've heard the rumors," I say. "Where were you and your husband the night Sterling was murdered."

"You have got to be kidding," she says. "Avery was Jamie's meal ticket."

"Or was, until Orson Welles entered the picture."

"Get real," she scoffs. "Welles was Avery's wet dream and Jamie knew it."

"You still haven't answered my question. Where were you last Tuesday night?"

"We were at the friggin' ballet!" she responds with all the gentility of a longshoreman.

"Okay, okay," I say trying to calm her down. Passersby are starting to stare at us.

"I just told you who killed Avery. Check it out, then tell the cop."

"I will," I say. "Absolutely."

She humphs at me in disgust, pushes her glasses up into their proper position and walks away, striding toward a shiny new Cadillac at the curb halfway up the block. I watch as she circles around to the driver's side door and begins to search her purse for her car keys. I go into the building and then decide to look back to make sure she's gone. I watch as she leaves the Caddy and walks across the street to a beat up old Plymouth station wagon where she gets in and drives away.

CHAPTER FOURTEEN

I get lucky. Between Glenda Mae and Bert they are able to concoct a diversion that allows me to slip into my private office unobserved and when I finally appear at around ten minutes to two, Oscar is none the wiser for my absence. Glenda Mae had ordered him a ham on rye to go with my pastrami so he is not ravenous. I have a pastrami sandwich on my desk which I will leave for the cleaning guy. Waste not, want not. I make one more impassioned plea to Oscar to go back to Jake Silver's place but he won't budge. His orders are very clear, I have this feeling that if I were to take a header out of my tenth floor window, Oscar would be right behind me.

My afternoon is one part irritation, one part aggravation and one part frustration. I get a call from Marco Conti who invites me to dinner. He thinks we should get together to cement our relationship. I tell him we have no relationship and if he doesn't stop bandying my name about in these union-management contract talks, I am going to turn him over to Miguel, an aspiring actor and a viper of a hood from the barrio who handles a knife like Tommy Dorsey handles a trombone. Miguel will not be impressed by Conti's ties to an East Coast gang of Sicilians. He will gut him like a fish. I feel good that I've made my position crystal clear. Conti says he will check in with me tomorrow. Maybe we can do lunch.

Fifteen minutes later Bill Goetz is on the phone. He runs Universal- International and he has heard in a roundabout way that I am involved in the scurrilous attack on the studio that appeared in Phineas' newspaper column. He reminds me that the studio has the right to do any damned thing it pleases with Welles' film, that what they are doing is only making it better, and that I would be well-advised to mind my own business because if I don't I am going to be hearing from U-I's legal department. I love chatting with Bill, we get to do it so seldom. It's a highlight of my afternoon.

I still haven't come to grips with the Bunny situation and it's been eating at me ever since my call to Ocala. Finally I can't stand it any more and I call my good pal, Mick Clausen. He runs a very successful bail bond business and has been married to my ex-wife Lydia for the last eight years. They have four kids. One of them is named for me.

When I get him on the line, he cheerily asks me what's up. I tell him about Bunny.

"Oh, shit," he says, his voice going flat and dark.

"I thought maybe you could put one of your people on it, Mick. Money's no object."

"Joe, you've been here before, remember? Those two private eyes you hired a few years back and drained you, giving you nothing in return."

"This'll be different, Mick," I tell him.

"Joe, she's in the wind. You gotta face it, man. The closer she gets to normalcy and responsibility, the more unstable she becomes."

"Maybe. Maybe not. I need you, Mick. Please."

There's a long pause and I think I hear sigh.

"Okay. Right now I haven't got anybody I can spare but Kim Patterson'll be back from Colorado on Wednesday. I can put him right on it if it's what you really want."

"It is."

"Okay, I'll have him call you. And Joe, take some advice. Pray for the best, expect the worst."

"Right," I say. "Love to Lydia and the kids."

"Sure," Mick says and hangs up.

I lean back in my chair and stare up at the ceiling. I suppose things could be worse but I don't know how. Jake Silver wants to kill me, Detective Ciello wants to arrest me and Bill Goetz wants to sue me. Worse, Bunny has run off somewhere and coincidentally so has a guy who used to work with Bunny at the Globe. My sharply aware brain cells tell me these two events are connected. At times they also tell me that ice is cold and fire is hot. I am a very perceptive fellow. To add to my troubles I have a colossus in a cheap suit sitting out on my sofa who insists he is going home with me tonight and I can't think of a safe way to dissuade him.

At that moment Glenda Mae buzzes me. I pick up.

"A gentleman out here to see you,sir. He doesn't have an appointment."

"Is he packing heat?" I ask.

"Not so's I can notice," she says.

"He give a name?"

"He gave me his card. His name is James Brennan Kreitzmann, Auteur. Either he writes dirty French novels or he's a director nobody ever heard of."

"Fine instincts, my girl. Have him come in."

I hang up and sit back, awaiting Jamie Kreitzmann's entrance. When it comes it's a dilly. I put him in his late 40's or early 50's, thinning hair, ruddy complexion, a neatly trimmed beard and mustache. He is wearing a custom tailored three-piece suit, a muted olive and gold striped tie with a show handkerchief to match and in his lapel, a white carnation boutonniere. He makes Adolphe Menjou look like a slug from a soup kitchen.

"Mr. Bernardi, how gracious of you to see me," he says, mincing his way to my desk, smelling like lavender, hand extended. I'm not sure if I'm supposed to shake it or kiss it. I do neither.

"I'm extremely busy this afternoon, Mr. Kreitzmann, but I can spare you a few minutes. Please sit down." I gesture to the chair that sits on the other side of my desk. I try to picture this guy in bed with the glamorous Pauline. The image eludes me.

"I understand my wife accosted you earlier today. I am here to apologize," Kreitzmann says.

"Not necessary," I say.

"She made accusations against Miss McBride. Unfounded. Also unseemly. We are all saddened by Avery's passing but it does no good to cast suspicion on friends and co-workers. Determining who killed our much loved friend is a job for the police."

I nod, my gaze fixed on Kreitzmann's white carnation.

"Do you always wear a flower in your lapel?" I ask him.

"I do."

"Is it always a white carnation?"

"What's my boutonniere got to do with anything? You are off the subject, Mr. Bernardi."

"Then I'll get right back on," I reply. "When you say that Sterling was much loved, may I assume you are talking about your wife?"

Kreitzmann smiles.

"Both Pauline and Avery were people with healthy sexual appetites," he says. "His death has been a severe blow to her."

"Then you knew your wife was sleeping with the guy."

"Knew it? I condoned it. I encouraged it," Kreitzmann says adamantly.

"So you could get ahead."

"So WE could get ahead, Mr, Bernardi. I am a brilliant director with several excellent B movie credits but I have yet to make that leap into the ranks of the elite like Hitchcock and Wyler and Ford.

Pauline has aspirations of her own. She, too, would like to produce and direct but with the exception of Ida Lupino, even the most talented of women are shut out from those opportunities. Working as a team we felt we could reach our goals more quickly."

"Then yours isn't really a marriage, it's a business arrangement."

"It is most certainly a legal marriage, sir, but we are both free to choose our bed partners without guilt or recrimination."

I nod, leaning back in my chair. This is no surprise, not really. Hollywood is rife with such arrangements to convince the moviegoing public that the most macho of their he-man idols are masculine through and through. Ditto their female counterparts, cuddly sex kittens on screen and as butch as Wallace Beery in the bedroom.

"Now let me get this straight," I say to him. "You made this special trip to see me just to apologize for your wife who, out of jealousy, unfairly accused Melanie McBride of murder."

"Not that alone,sir. I also want to correct the record. When you asked Pauline where we were at the time of Avery's death, she told you we were at the ballet. We were not. She meant to say that we are at the Art Classics Theater in West Hollywood, watching the twelve midnight showing of "The Red Shoes", a vintage movie ABOUT ballet."

"I know the picture," I say. "Norma Shearer and Anton Walburn."

Kreitzmann throws me a condescending look.

"Moira Shearer, not Norma Shearer. Mr. Bernardi," he says. "And there is no such person as Anton Walburn. The actor's name is Anton Walbrook, born Adolf Anton Wilhelm Wohlbruck in Vienna, Austria, in 1896."

"My mistake," I say. "Now about your alibi."

His eyes flare in indignation.

"I have just told you where Pauline and I were at the time of Avery's death. Did you know, sir, that my wife cried, yes, cried visibly at the end of the film in that particularly moving scene where

Vicky slips off the platform into the path of the oncoming train and then as she lies bloody and battered on the stretcher, begs Julian to remove her red shoes before she dies."

"Impressive," I say. "But less impressive when I recall that you have a photographic memory, especially about films you may have seen only once."

"Damn it, sir, what possible reason could we have for killing our dear friend? He was our path to fame and we both were intensely loyal to him. Two weeks ago I was offered a directorial assignment by a major studio. A lighthearted family comedy with Charles McGraw and Agnes Moorehead attached. I turned it down flat. There are still some of us in this business with a sense of loyalty and integrity."

"Yes, and I salute all five of you," I say.

He glares at me. "I'm afraid your cynicism is lost on me, Mr. Bernardi. In the interest of cooperation, I felt it important to clear up the minor matter of our whereabouts before you passed erroneous information on to the police detective in charge whoever that might be. Thank you for your time."

He turns and leaves the room. Whether he knows it or not this silly poppinjay has supplied me with some information, first and most important is his damned flower. That answers the question of who the carnation petals at the murder scene belong to. Next, it's almost certain that he and Pauline did not attend 'The Red Shoes". They may not have even attended the ballet which has been performing at the Pasadena Civic Auditorium for the past three weeks. Even if the performance let out as late as 10:30, highly unlikely, it's not much of an alibi for a murder committed at twelve midnight. Finally, more proof that Vito Ciello, Detective Second Grade, is a complete incompetent. Avery Sterling has been dead for six days and Ciello has yet to interview these two prime suspects. I have a feeling he hasn't really interviewed anyone except me.

At my wit's end, I get to my feet. I can't think any more. My wall clock reads 5:35 and I need a respite from all this. The only place I'll find it is at home. I walk out into my anteroom where the first thing I see is Oscar. I'd momentarily forgotten about him. He rises from the sofa and smiles.

"We go now?" he asks.

I hate to disappoint him.

"We go now," I reply.

I make it clear to him that, Jake Silver be damned, Oscar is not going to be a house guest. If he wants to sleep in his car, that's his problem and not mine. He says he understands completely. He follows me to Van Nuys in that big flashy Cadillac and after I have pulled into my driveway, he pulls in immediately behind me. If I plan on sneaking off tonight, I'll have to do it on foot. Oscar has me boxed in.

I walk to my side door that enters into the kitchen. I open it and look back at Oscar. He's like a big puppy dog staring at me. Not begging, just staring, and I know I won't be able to digest my dinner if I leave him sitting there behind the wheel. I wave at him to join me. He doesn't have to be asked twice.

Once inside he looks all around my comfortable yet humble abode and furrows his brow.

"I thought you were rich," he says to me.

"I'm saving my money for Armageddon," I reply.

"Who's she?" he asks.

I don't waste time trying to explain it.

"You like turkey?" I ask.

"Sure," he says.

I take two TV dinners out of the freezer section of my refrigerator. I make a show of looking at the instructions and finally hand one of them to Oscar.

"I can't read this. How long does this say to keep them in the oven?"

He looks, squints, and then squints even harder.

"I don't know," he says. "I can't read it either."

"Oscar, what happened to your glasses?" I ask.

"I think I lost them," he says.

"Lost them where?"

"I don't know. They were in my pocket and then they were gone."

I nod. Nothing to be gained by telling him where they were found, at least not yet. I stick the aluminum trays in the oven and set it at 425. In 25 minutes they'll be ready. I tell Oscar to go into the living room and watch television if he'd like. I go into the bedroom to freshen up and change clothes. I'm just slipping into my slacks and L.A. Dodgers T-shirt when the phone rings. I have spent a few bucks to have an extension put in the bedroom so I don't have to race to the kitchen every time it rings. I pick up.

"Hello."

"Joe, it's Orson Welles."

I am relieved to hear his voice.

"I'm glad to hear from you, Orson, Where are you?""

"Still in the Bahamas with Noel. I may be flying out shortly. I wanted to check in for the latest. Anything I should know about?"

"There's a warrant out for your arrest," I say.

"Preposterous," he says. "What else?"

I tell him about Ceillo's non-investigation.

"A dunderhead. I knew it the minute he opened his mouth."

"When you say you're flying out, Orson, does that mean you're returning to Los Angeles?"

"Oh no, dear fellow. If this new money man comes through I will be flying to the Canaries to scout locations for a movie version of 'The Tempest' which I will direct and also play Prospero. I have high hopes that Noel will agree to play Alonso. Well, give my best to Bertha and do keep in touch. Remember you have my whole-hearted support."

Whereupon he hangs up, leaving me to wonder just what form this support has taken or will take. In any case I have reached the irrefutable conclusion that Orson is a man that marches to a different drummer and more than that, he IS the drummer as well as the rest of the band rolled up into one bigger than life personality.

Time for dinner and I head for the kitchen. Oscar's watching Howdy Doody and enjoying it immensely. I can't believe the thing is still on the air after ten years but I guess new kids keep coming along to keep it alive. I bring Oscar his dinner and a TV tray to put it on so he won't have to miss a second of the entertainment. I choose to eat in the kitchen, far from the hilarity being foisted on the Peanut Gallery by Clarabelle, the Clown. By now I haven't the heart to send Oscar off to a night sitting in his car so I dig up a pillow and a blanket and tell him to make himself comfortable on the sofa. He smiles gratefully. He really is a big teddy bear.

After I eat I head for the bedroom, climb under the covers and dig into my nightstand drawer for my copy of 'Peyton Place'. No one in my position would be caught dead reading such trash so that is why I read it in the privacy of my bedroom. This is not unlike what several hundred other movers and shakers of the industry are doing. In fact the only honest man in Hollywood may be Jerry Wald at 20th who has paid handsomely for the movie rights and predicts he will make a fortune with it. He's probably right. You'll lose your shirt betting against Jerry Wald.

I am fascinated but my eyes grow heavy and by ten-thirty I've had enough. I return the book to the nightstand and flip off the light. Sleep grabs me immediately. I'm in the middle of a wet dream about Constance MacKenzie when my phone jars me awake. I look at the clock. Ten after midnight. This better not be a wrong number.

"Hello," I mutter.

"Joe?"

"Who wants to know?"

"It's Aaron, Joe. I'm just calling to see if you're at home."

"I'm home," I say. "Thanks for calling. I'll catch you later."

"Don't hang up, Joe. I've got a corpse on my hands."

I bring the receiver back to my ear.

"Anybody I know?"

"Well, his name may be Ryan Walker or it may be Joel Walberg but either way, they're both dead."

CHAPTER FIFTEEN

Joel Walberg's house in Reseda is no more than twenty minutes away. I hop into my clothes and head for the kitchen. Oscar needed no wakening. He had been watching Steve Allen on one of the local channels. I tell him what happened and he insists on following me over there. All I want is for him to move the Caddy so I can back out but he's adamant. Where I go, he goes, which is why when I pull up to the curb a couple of houses down from Joel Walberg's place, Oscar pulls in right behind me.

As I stride toward Joel's house, I jostle a few Looky Lous who have gathered to watch the festivities, and stride past the two squad cars and the city meat wagon. No press. Not yet but they won't be far behind. Lou Cioffi will be among them. Like a vampire, Lou works the mean streets by night and sleeps by day.

Oscar is hot on my tail as I duck under the yellow police crime scene tape and head for the front door. The tape doesn't dissuade Oscar. He presses forth. At the front door a uniformed cop attempts to stop me.

"My name's Bernardi. Lt. Kleinschmidt sent for me. "

The cop checks a list on a clipboard he's carrying.

"Yes, sir. Go right in." But even as he is saying it, he grabs my arm. "What about the guy behind you?" he asks quietly.

I look back over my shoulder.

"Go back to your car, Oscar,"I say. "You can't come in here."

He glowers and for a minute I think he's going to try to bull his way in. But then he turns around and walks away.

"Bodyguard?" the cop asks.

"I don't know yet. Maybe."

I walk through the front door into the living room. It is quiet as it always is at crime scenes. Professionals busy doing their jobs with a minimum of chatter. A corpse is a corpse. They see them all the time.

Pete Rodriguez emerges from one of the bedrooms. Our eyes meet. Instant recognition. I walk over to him, hand extended. We shake.

"How the hell are you, Pete?" I ask.

"Never better, Joe," he says.

"What are you doing here? You got a robbery to go along with the homicide?"

Four years ago, Rodriguez was a Detective Third working out of the Van Nuys Division. We worked together on a case involving an actor who had disappeared from a movie set with foul play a possibility.

"Nope. Passed the Sergeant's exam and got transferred to Homicide. I knew right away this one had something to do with that movie producer killing so I called Aaron. He's in the bedroom with the stiff. I know he wants to talk to you."

I nod and congratulate him on his promotion. I know for a fact he has no rabbi. He earned that sergeant's shield all by himself. I walk over to the bedroom door and peer in. It has been set up as an office. Joel Walberg's body is splayed awkwardly in his office chair. Part of his skull is missing. There is blood spatter everywhere. Lying on the floor just below his right hand is an ugly looking pistol. The police photographer is shooting the body from every angle. The print guy is dusting a nearby bookshelf and Aaron is kneeling down using a penknife to get scrapings from under Joel's fingernails. He looks up and sees me and waves me in. I move closer which is when I notice the letter in Joel's typewriter. Not a letter really. More like a note

"The next door neighbor heard what she thought was a gunshot at around ten-thirty," Aaron says. "She sent her husband over to the investigate. When no one answered the doorbell, he started to circle the house, looking in windows. That's when he spotted Walberg like this."

I point to the typewriter.

"Suicide note?"

"Looks like it."

"Mind if I read it?"

"Read. Don't touch," Aaron says.

I ease over to the desk, putting my hands behind my back. I lean forward and read.

The end is at hand. I freely admit that I killed him but
honour demands that I declare that I and I alone am
responsible. I am done with pain and done with fear.
At long last, farewell to a world that will have none of me.
Weep not. I take this step gladly.

Aaron says, "That sound like a suicide note to you, Joe? Sounds like one to me, even if it is a little flowery."

"He didn't sign it," I say.

"Lots of times they don't," Aaron tells me.

"Ciello's going to take one look at this and close the Sterling case," I say.

"And why not?" Aaron asks.

"Because this is bullshit. I spent over an hour with the guy on Saturday and he was anything but suicidal. He was funny, verbose, upbeat."

"Didn't you tell me he'd been blacklisted, that he couldn't find work?"

"Not in the movie business. Not under his real name. But he told me he was working on a play for Broadway. He already had an advance from Jake Shubert. Why would the guy kill himself?"

"Fear. Shame. Guilt. You name it."

"This is all wrong, Aaron. Where's his peepers?"

"His what?"

"Peepers. Glasses."

"What glasses?"

"He wore thick-lensed reading glasses for close work. He couldn't have typed that note without them."

"I didn't see any glasses," Aaron says.

I turn and go out into the kitchen. On the table I find the manuscript. On the manuscript I find his reading glasses. I take them back into the small bedroom and hand them to Aaron.

"He'd been proofreading at the kitchen table," I say.

Aaron examines them carefully, then slips them into one of the small manila envelopes he always carries in his jacket pocket.

"It'd be a lot safer for you, Joe, if you let Ciello close this case," Aaron says quietly.

"Maybe so, Aaron, and if the only corpse was Avery Sterling, I might look the other way. But I liked this man and I admired him and I'm pretty damned sure somebody killed him and I'm not going to back off."

Aaron gets to his feet, shaking his head.

"You've got a moral compass that I should admire, Joe, but I'm scared to death that one of these days it's going to get you killed."

"So I keep telling myself," I say ruefully.

"How about if you and I talk to Ciello, tell him what we think and let him carry on from there," Aaron says.

"You're kidding," I say.

"You're not a cop, Joe. Don't act like one."

"I'm not stupid, Aaron. I'm not going to do anything crazy. But this, this isn't right."

I turn and head for the door. I hear Aaron call my name. I turn. He looks at me and then finally, in resignation, he shakes his head and waves me away.

It doesn't take long for Detective Second Grade Vito Ciello to take the bait. By eight o'clock he has been told of the so-called suicide in Reseda. The hook is set by nine-thirty when he announces a press conference will be held at eleven o'clock and at eleven sharp at a large meeting room at Central Division, he announces to the world that the killer of Avery Sterling, up and coming young Hollywood producer, has been identified. I am in my office, watching this drivel on my 10" television set which is mounted into one of my bookcases. Joel Walberg is described as a deranged writer, exposed by the House Un-American Activities Committee as a Communist sympathizer. He had been working for the victim under an assumed name as a properties evaluator. His exact motive for killing his employer has not yet been determined but is under investigation. Ciello preens like a peacock for the television cameras as well as members of the print press. I feel sick.

At twelve noon I receive two visitors in my office. Jake Silver extends his hand.

"I owe you an apology, Mr. Bernardi. I was wrong about you and I am a big enough man to admit when I've made a mistake."

Douglas Webster, who has accompanied Silver to my office, is apparently not that big a man. He stands mute behind his employer, looking at me with cold steely eyes.

The jewelry mogul and I shake hands and I thank him for his

honesty. He tells me that my life is no longer threatened. If this means that Marco Conti must return to New York immediately, so be it. He was always uncomfortable dealing with the Gambinos. He will not do it again. He also expresses hope that I was not badly inconvenienced by Oscar's presence. I tell him I was not.

Silver smiles.

"You are a mensch, Mr. Bernardi. I will keep this in mind for the future. Meanwhile I bid you goodbye. If ever there is some small thing I can do for you, do not hesitate to ask."

It is a wonderful moment, full of warmth and good cheer. I decide to destroy it.

"And if it turns out that Joel Walberg did not kill your son, that he was killed by someone else?"

The old man looks at me curiously.

"You're crazy," Webster snarls.

"Am I?" I stare him down.

"Are you talking about Roy Watson, the gonef who has been robbing us blind for the past year?"

"I don't know. Am I?"

"We plan on dealing with Watson in our own way," Webster says.

"Well, that's just fine. Put a bullet behind his ear and dump him in the ocean off Zuma Beach and you'll never know if he was the one who killed Avrom," I say.

"You think the police have made a mistake," Jake Silver says.

"I think it's possible."

"But you're not sure."

"You mean, do I have proof? No, I don't, but I'm going to do my best to find it. Do I have your blessing?"

He hesitates, looking into my eyes.

"You do," he says.

"And if it turns out to be someone close to you, Mr. Silver?" My eyes shift instinctively to Douglas Webster. Silver catches it.

"My dead son deserves the truth, whatever that may be, Mr. Bernardi. Do what you have to do. You will not be interfered with."

He turns and goes to the door. Webster looks at me. The cold expression on his face speaks volumes. After a moment he follows the old man out of my office. They pick up Oscar on the way and the three of them leave. I wonder if Jake Silver meant what he said. I have a gut feeling he did.

CHAPTER SIXTEEN

If I am to get to the bottom of Joel Walberg's murder, I'm going to need help and I am certainly not going to get it from Detective Second Grade Vito Ciello. It's nearing one o'clock and that means Lou Cioffi is having breakfast at Danny Shea's Black Shillelagh, a disreputable bar and grill a block away from the *Times* building. I decide to go spoil his appetite. Before I head out the door I ask Glenda Mae to call Melanie and get an address and a phone number for Roy Watson. For all I know he may be in the pokey already but if not he deserves to know that evildoers are on his trail.

I drive down to West 1st Street mulling over what I know and it's precious little. Someone killed Avery Sterling, most likely shooting him with the same pistol that was found next to Joel Walberg's dead hand. If you are going to frame a corpse for a murder that you have committed, it helps to provide the proper murder weapon. Something else to think about. The killer shot Sterling twice to mask motive. A shot to the head is one thing. A bullet to a man's private parts is quite another. It spells womanhood. Melanie McBride? Pauline Kreitzmann? Henny Hanks? Was the murder committed by one of them or was the bullet fired into Avery's manhood a distraction? To further cast suspicion on a wide range of suspects, the killer salted the crime scene with enough clues to fill an anthology of Sherlock Holmes. He or she was obviously hoping that, in a sea of clues, his or her motive and identity would be sufficiently masked. So far, he or she is right.

But in creating this mountain of conflicting clues, the killer has made a mistake. He did not count on an intellectually impaired investigating detective who would immediately fixate on two people who could not by any stretch of the imagination be considered suspects, particularly Orson Welles. Under ordinary circumstances this would be a three paragraph story on page 21. After all, Avery Sterling was not David O. Selznick but suddenly, under intense scrutiny by the press because of Orson Welles' celebrity, all the phony red herrings were liable to be exposed for what they were. Suddenly a flesh and blood killer was desperately needed, an irrefutable fall guy whose corpse would take the blame and allow the murder of Avery Sterling to be closed and disappear from view. Joel Walberg, certified Communist and Jewish to boot, fit the profile perfectly.

I park on the street and feed the meter a couple of dimes. When I walk into the bar, it takes a moment for my eyes to adjust to the darkness. There are shadows everywhere and it's noisy but after a moment I spot Lou at the end of the bar cracking open a hard boiled egg. A tankard of Guiness is at his elbow. I slip onto the stool beside him. He looks up and recognizes me.

"Jesus," he says, "they'll let anybody in here."

"I was about to say the same thing," I reply.

"Had breakfast? The eggs are great."

I look over at the basket of hard-boiled eggs in the middle of the bar with its little handwritten sign, "Take One".

"Do you newspaper people ever pay for anything?" I ask.

"On our salaries? Get real, Joe."

I signal the bartender. He comes over and I order a Coors in the bottle. When he walks off to get it, I say to Lou, "You see Ciello's press conference this morning?"

"While I was shaving. I can't believe it. The dumb bastard got lucky."

"Makes a better story if he didn't," I say enigmatically.

Lou looks at me curiously. Just then my Coors arrives and I take a long pull on the bottle.

"What do you know that I don't?" he asks.

"Off the record?"

"Sure."

"Walberg's suicide was staged. Sterling's killer iced him to get the Sterling case closed."

"You can prove that?"

"No, but it fits. Walberg wasn't suicidal. Anything but. I can't be quoted. Neither can Aaron."

"Kleinschmidt?"

"He'll give you everything you need off the record. Then you dig."

"On the level?"

"The word from the bird," I say.

We chat for a few minutes more and I finish my beer but I got what I came for. Lou is hooked. Tomorrow's edition will cover Ciello's press conference but Lou will hint at doubts. The following day he'll start to lay out the case that Walberg may have been killed. By Friday he'll have Ciello looking dumber than Clem Kadiddlehopper even as the real killer starts to get very, very nervous.

I say goodbye to Lou as he reaches for a second hardboiled egg and go in search of a phone booth. Glenda Mae has dug up the phone number and address for Roy Watson. I consider calling him but change my mind. I want to look in the guy's eyes when I warn him about Douglas Webster.

Watson lives in a rundown apartment house on Fairfax a couple of blocks from the Farmer's Market. I buzz his ground floor unit and after a few seconds, his voice comes over the intercom.

"Yeah, who is it?"

"Joe Bernardi."

"What do you want?"

"We need to talk."

"Go away."

"Sure, if that's what you want. I'll look up the guys who are out to kill you and tell them where they can find you."

There's a moment of silence and then a buzz at the door. I turn the handle and walk inside to a dimly lit foyer. Watson's unit, 1F, is at the end of the corridor and I start down toward it. Before I get there, the door opens and Watson appears. He's wearing white boxer shorts, an open terry cloth robe and black socks on his feet. In his right hand he is holding a revolver.

"Why the gun?" I ask when I reach him.

"Why not?" he says, stepping aside to let me in. He takes one last look down the corridor, then follows me in and closes and bolts the door.

"Safety first," I say.

"You got that right," he says.

One of the bedroom doors is open and I notice that the light coming from the room is exceptionally bright.

"What are you doing in there?" I smile facetiously. "Shooting a movie?"

Before he can answer, a girl comes out of the room. She can't be more than twenty years old and she's wearing a see-through negligee. That's all she's wearing.

"C'mon, Roy, are we gonna shoot this friggin' thing or aren't we? My knees are killing me."

"We're taking thirty for lunch, babe. Tell the guys. Food's in the kitchen."

"Yeah. Cold pizza," she says. "I've been looking forward to it all day." She goes back into the bedroom and in a moment, the light goes out and a moment or two after that, she and six guys troop out of the room and head for the kitchen in back.

"Are you filming what I think you're filming?" I ask.

"Sure. Good money in this stuff. The distributors'll buy anything we shoot. We'll never play Grauman's or win an Oscar but we cash a lot of checks."

"Aren't you afraid the other tenants will complain?"

"No. Their rent's cheap and we own the building. Besides, some of them I use in the pictures. We have no problems."

"That's twice you've said 'we'. Who's we?" I ask.

"I'm not sure that's any of your business," Watson says.

"Two people are dead and I can have the cops all over this place inside of two hours. That makes it my business," I tell him.

He hesitates, trying to figure my angle.

"Sure. Why not? Me, Doug Webster and Henny Hanks. And Avery before he died."

"But not Jake Silver."

"Not Jake Silver," Watson says. "The old man provided the start up cash when he funded Avery's production company. For the past year we've been coining money and we're in the process of putting back everything we took out because we knew that sooner or later the old man would be checking the books."

"A perfect setup," I say. "You and Webster start getting rich, Henny starts putting aside rainy day money because 5% of the old man's estate wasn't going to pay a lot of bills. But then all of a sudden Avery is dead. What happened?"

Watson looks at me with a wry grin, then walks over to a nearby table and takes a cigarette from a fancy enameled box. He lights up.

"What happened? Avery decided he wanted to make a movie, that's what happened," Watson says. "The dumb jerk wanted to shut down this gold mine and put up the cash to make a real movie.

you know, the kind with a story and special effects and wardrobe, particularly wardrobe because mostly the actors were going to keep their clothes on."

"That couldn't have made you very happy," I say.

"Yeah, and not only me but Doug and especially Henny who was spitting nails. When the kid first went to Jake for the money to start his production company, Jake turned him down. But Henny was already thinking ahead. It was Henny who got Jake to change his mind and then when Avery wanted to turn everything upside down to finance some friggin' movie about marathon dancers, she went crazy."

"Crazy enough to kill him?" I ask.

That brings Watson up short.

"Henny kill him? No, I never thought it was Henny."

"But you did think it could have been Doug Webster."

"I didn't say that," Watson says.

"You ever consider maybe Webster believes it was you?"

He glares at me and then crushes out his cigarette in a big brass ashtray,

"Why are you here, Mr. Bernardi?" he asks.

"A fool's errand, Mr. Watson. I came to warn you that your partner is under orders to find you and, what was the phrase, deal with you. Naturally that's not going to happen. He is, after all, your partner. Unless, of course, he wants to make Brownie points with his employer and after all, with you out of the way, he gets a bigger piece of the action. But pay no attention to me, Mr. Watson. I'm just ruminating. Sorry to have interrupted your filming."

I start to leave. When my hand is on the doorknob, Watson says to me,"Mr. Bernardi. I am going to assume that you will keep everything you have seen here to yourself."

"I'll try," I say cheerily.

"To do otherwise might prove unhealthy," Watson says. "I'm

sure you find that obvious."

I look at him with a smile.

"Not only obvious, but elementary, my dear Watson."

I couldn't resist.

It's late when I get back to the office. Nothing's going on. Glenda Mae is getting ready to leave and I have one call which I return immediately.

"Kleinschmidt," he says on the other end of the line.

"It's me," I say.

"Well, glad to see you're still alive," he says. "Got it all sorted out yet?"

"Not quite. How about you?"

"None of your business. What do you want?"

"You called me. I'm returning your call."

"Oh, yeah. The coroner came through. Finally," Aaron says. "Got a pencil and paper?"

I grab a pencil from my caddy and take a sheet of Hammermill from my desk drawer.

"Shoot."

"Avery Sterling autopsy. Cause of death, GSW to the head. The shot to his balls came first. Probably hurt like hell but wasn't fatal. The second shot was between the eyes. That's the one that did him in."

"Check."

"Two slugs found in body. Both 9mm. Ballistics analysis confirms that the gun used to kill Sterling was the weapon found at the scene of the Walberg suicide, a Browning HP 9 mm, unregistered and untraceable."

"No surprise there," I say.

"Ciello takes that as proof positive that Walberg killed Sterling."

"And if proves to me that Walberg was framed. Last night at the crime scene something was bothering me and I couldn't figure out what it was and as I was driving downtown to talk to Lou

Cioffi, it came to me. The gun. You found it on the floor beneath Walberg's right hand."

"That's right."

"So the gunshot was to his right temple."

"Right again. So what?"

"I spent over an hour with the guy. We drank coffee at his kitchen table and chatted about everything from Charles Boyer's hairpiece to the folly of 3D movies."

"And?"

"And when he poured the coffee from the coffee pot he was holding it in his left hand."

A moment of silence.

"Point made, Joe. Anything else new on your end?" he asks.

An image of the babe in the see-through negligee crosses my mind.

"Nothing a homicide detective has to get involved with," I say.

"Is that right? I slap suspects around when they give me an answer like that one."

"I'll tell you when I can, Aaron. If I tell you now, you'd have to make an arrest and that might seriously screw up our chances of finding the killer."

"Okay. Then I'll go along. Has Jake Silver called off his goons or are you still on his hit list?"

"He tells me I'm okay."

"Good. I'll notify the guys at Vice so they can deal with Marco Conti. So now there's no compelling reason you should be involved in any of this."

"Not really."

"But you're not going to quit, are you?"

"No, I'm not."

"I'll send flowers," Aaron says and hangs up.

CHAPTER SEVENTEEN

It's dark when I leave the office for home. It's only six o'clock but November's like that. Winter will soon be upon us. Minnesota will be buried under yards of snow and not come up for air until April. Here in Los Angeles, it just gets chilly and it's chilly now. The temperature reading on the nearby bank building is 52. In downtown L.A. that's frostbite time. Normally I'd drive by Jill's to spend a few minutes with Yvette but Jill says she's come down with a cold and is propped up in bed milking her illness for all it's worth. Maybe tomorrow, Jill says.

Traffic is still heavy and the going is slow and I'm enjoying drive-time on my car radio. Two goofballs whose names I didn't get are spinning Pat Boone's 'Love Letters in the Sand' and one guy says it was stolen from something by Chopin and the other guy says it was written in the 1880's under the title "The Spanish Cavalier" and dodos from Hawaiian Gardens to Bakersfield are calling in with their two cents worth. It's totally stupid and absolutely hilarious. If I hadn't been laughing so hard I might have noticed that a two-toned Ford Fairlane had been on my tail ever since I left the parking lot.

Once I get over the hill I turn onto Ventura Boulevard and then swing north onto White Oak. Traffic's still heavy so I opt for a short-cut by turning right onto Collins Street which is quiet and residential.

For the first time I notice the Fairlane and I notice him because he is behind me, his headlights glaring in my rearview mirror, and he's roaring up toward me like we're on the Daytona Speedway. He pulls alongside and slows. There are no street lights on Collins so I can't see who's behind the wheel. I also can't see who is in the back seat but I do see the gloved hand and the pistol jutting out of the open window and instinctively I duck and swerve, just as the gun is fired and a bullet blasts through my window, missing me by inches.

My Bentley is momentarily out of control and I fight to keep it from tipping over as it skids sideways along the pavement. It jumps the curb and my head slams forward into the windshield. Even though I am dazed, I can see up ahead as the Fairlane stops and then begins to turn around. I know he's coming back for a second try. It's then I realize that the engine has quit. I turn the key and pump the gas. The starter struggles but the engine won't turn over. I'm up over the curb at a 45 degree angle, dead in the water. The Fairlane has turned now and is heading back toward me. I have seconds to act.

I pop open the glove box and take out my .25 Beretta automatic and in one motion I smash the map light attached to the rear view mirror. I make sure the safety is off and then, ducking down, I open my door which is hidden from the Fairlane's view and in the darkness slide out onto the sidewalk. I get to my feet and crouch behind the engine compartment, holding the pistol with both hands. The Fairlane creeps to a stop next to my car and at that point, I rise up and pump four shots directly at the passenger side window. Even as I am firing, the Fairlane lays a patch and is flying down the street away from me.

"Hey, what's going on out here?" A man's voice.

I look. He's standing in the doorway of his house, staring out at me. I turn and start toward him. I manage to get out, "Call the police!" before I stumble forward, blood pouring from a head wound into my eyes. A black rain cloud appears in my brain getting darker and darker and then I pass out.

When I wake up I find myself in a hospital emergency room. It is brightly lit, smells fresh and clean, everything is white and well scrubbed and a placard on a far wall reads Valley Presbyterian Hospital. I remember reading about this place in the Valley News. It just opened this year and is getting rave reviews from Valleyites.

A white coated woman is standing a few feet away leaning over a medical tray,

"Oh, Nurse," I say.

She turns to me with a smile.

"That's Doctor, Mr. Bernardi, and I am glad to see you awake."

Her accent's as British as shepherd's pie and on her it sounds good. The name tag pinned to her starched white blouse says 'Gwendolyn Collier, M.D."

"What are my chances?" I ask her.

"Of what?"

"Survival."

She eyes me thoughtfully.

"That depends upon what the cardiologist says. He'll be here as soon as you're done with the proctologist whom I expect to pop by any moment."

I laugh. She laughs with me.

"Then I needn't put my affairs in order."

"Not at the moment." She takes a very large thermometer from her tray. "Roll over on your side," she says.

"Oh, now wait a minute," I say. "How about an oral thermometer?"

"Unreliable," she replies and pushes at my hip. I feel in odd sensation as my rectum gets violated. Now I have no secrets from this woman.

"Usually when a woman gets this intimate with me, she buys

me a beer first."

"I thought of that but there's no alcohol permitted in hospital."

"THE hospital," I correct her.

"No, that's what you Yanks say. We English are more civilised and that's civilised with an 's'. not a zed."

"Sorry, Doc, but you talk funny. I adore it but it's funny."

"The term, Mr. Bernardi, is The Queen's English, not Eisenhower's English. The lack of communication during the war was so abhorrent, I'm surprised that we won. Tell me, do you not like the English?"

"I love them," I say. "I own a Bentley, complete with bonnet, boot and glove box and tyres with a 'y'."

"Well done. There's hope for you yet."

"Thanks but you will never get me to put in an 's' where a 'z' belongs or a superfluous 'u' in flavor or harbor or a hundred others words that have delusions of grandeur. And by the way, don't you think it's time you removed that candy cane from my bum?"

"You're learning, Mr. Bernardi," she grins, yanking it out. She peers at it thoughtfully and her face clouds up.

"Oh, dear," she says. "Your temperature is way below normal."

"How much below?" I ask nervously.

"You're registering thirty-seven degrees."

"What!"

"Celsius."

"What does that mean?"

"It means you're going to live and as soon as I sew up that nasty gash just below your hairline, you can go."

She puts the thermometer back in the tray and picks up a needle of major league proportions.

"This may sting a bit," she says sweetly.

A few minutes later, I say bye-bye. She says ta-ta and I head out to the waiting room where I find Detective Pete Rodriguez. He admires my bandage. I tell him if he likes it so much, he can have it. He takes me by the arm and leads me over to a pair of side-by-side chairs at the back of the room.

"Okay," he says. "What happened out there on Collins? From the beginning?"

I do as I'm told and he listens intently.

"By the way," he asks. "Have you got a permit for that pea-shooter of yours?"

"I keep it in the glove box."

"What are you, English all of a sudden?" he asks giving me a fishy look. I explain the car's English, not me.

"When we finish here, I'll take a look. One of the boys got your car started. It's out in the parking lot."

I say "Thanks."

"I don't suppose you got a look at those two guys."

"Too dark. Coulda been two guys or a guy and a girl or even two babes."

"Okay, who had a motive to take you out?"

"Aside from everybody?" I ask politely. "What about the car?"

"Stolen from a parking lot at the May Company. We found it about six blocks from where you were jumped. We'll dust it for prints but didn't you tell me whoever was in the back seat wore gloves?" I nod ruefully. "Okay, have you got a safe place to stay tonight, and don't say your place because that isn't safe."

"I don't think they'll try again," I say.

"You don't think. Damned right you don't think. You came close to being blown away this evening, my friend, and for whatever reason, they may be desperate enough to keep on trying until they succeed."

I think of Jill and of Julio who lives at the house twenty-four hours a day with his .45 automatic and the security system that would rat out a curious mole trying to breach the perimeter. I excuse myself and go in search of a phone. When Jill answers I tell her the situation and she tells me to come right over. I return to Pete and tell him I'm covered for the rest of the night. I give him Jill's number in case he needs me and start off. He tags along and when we get to the Bentley, he puts out his hand for my gun permit. He scans it and hands it back. Pete Rodriguez cuts corners for nobody. He does, however, provide a police escort over to Jill's imposing house on Highland Avenue where I park at curbside.

Jill greets me at the front door and I wave goodbye to the squad car that was tailing me. I give her a hug and a kiss on the cheek and we go inside. Bridget, the housekeeper, has made up the guest bedroom for me and laid out a fresh pair of pajamas. She knows I sleep in my skivvies but she insists on the pajamas anyway so when I get up in the morning, I rumple them up and toss them on the floor. This seems to make the old girl's day.

"The kid still awake?" I ask.

"When she heard you were coming, I had no choice. She's doing Camille for us and her performance is first rate. Act impressed."

We climb the stairs and I pop my head into Yvette's bedroom. She is sitting up, coloring, with a sizable rag doll at her side. When she looks up and sees me, she immediately goes into a coughing jag.

"Oh, that sounds terrible," I say.

Very seriously she tells me, "I'm very sick."

"I can see that," I say, just as seriously.

We chat about the state of her health for a couple of minutes and then to get off the subject I ask about the rag doll at her side.

"This is Brighton Beach Bertie," she tells me. "He's British."

My God, I think, what is going on? Are we undergoing some sort of stealth attack by the Brits to retake the country. First Dr. Gwendolyn, now Yvette.

"He looks like a rat," I say.

"He's a hedgehog," Yvette replies. "And he talks."

She holds him up and squeezes him around the middle.

"Cheerio, old chap," says the doll.

"Lovely." I say.

She squeezes him again.

"I've got sixpence, 'ow about you?"

We go through Bertie's limited repertoire which I marvel at.

"You must be better, Yvette. You're not coughing as much," I say.

She immediately starts coughing again.

I suggest it's probably sleep time and Jill seconds my motion. I wave from the doorway as Jill tucks her in and douses her light. Whatever Dr. Gwendolyn gave me for pain is starting to wear off and I can't wait to climb under the covers and get some sleep. I give Jill an affectionate hug and make my way to my bedroom.

Luckily I get to sleep right away, dreaming of Winston Churchill who is pacing about a huge library and shaking a fist at me and telling me to mind my own business and when I ask what I've done wrong, he keeps shaking that fist and I can't shut him up.

It's exactly twenty minutes to six when I suddenly sit bolt upright in bed, struck by a thought I should have had days ago. At 38 the brain does not function as smoothly as it once did but better late than never. I can't get back to sleep and I toss and turn, knowing there is someplace I must go as soon as possible.

CHAPTER EIGHTEEN

I try to escape the house before everyone is up and about. No such luck. Jill has been up and down more times than the elevators at the Capitol Records Tower and when she's not busy checking on my little girl, Bridget is up and about doing her share. I was almost to the front door when Bridget spotted me and ordered me to the kitchen for breakfast. I acquiesce but not before I snatch the morning *L.A.Times* from the doorstep. I need to catch up on Phineas's Holy War against Universal-International regarding the Welles Affair.

I am searching for Phineas's column when Bridget shoves orange juice and coffee in my direction while asking how I would like my eggs. I figure "Non-existent" is not a satisfactory response so I settle for scrambled. Phineas has outdone himself with today's column which he has entitled 'The Booby and the Best'. He starts by deftly outlining Orson's many theatrical and motion picture accomplishments. He follows these with a short compendium of Vito Ciello's record as a policeman, laying heavy emphasis on Vito's powerful uncle at Parker Center. In short Vito Ciello is portrayed as an inept by-the-book-cop, in over his head and who, but for his uncle, would have been booted off the force months ago. How dare this non-entity even consider accusing Orson Welles of murder and on the subject of incompetents, how dare Universal permit dollar a day hack editors to mangle Orson Welles' latest masterpiece? Having humiliated Ciello and given a black eye to U-I's highhanded methods in dealing with proven movie geniuses, I can only wonder what my friend has in store for tomorrow's edition.

As Bridget slides my plate of eggs under my nose, Jill enters the kitchen looking like a scarecrow without stuffing, gaunt with dark circles under her eyes. She is plainly exhausted which she demonstrates by yawning widely as she sits down at the table.

"The princess is asleep," she announces.

"And you should be," I say. "You look like hell."

"I sure do," she says.

Bridget brings her the same orange juice and coffee she foisted on me a few minutes earlier. Jill opens a bottle which is sitting on a tray on the table and pops three pills into her mouth.

"What's that?" I ask.

"Iron. For my anemia."

"Says Dr. Dumbbunny?"

"He knows what he's doing."

"That's what they said about Custer. Do you feel any better?"

"Absolutely."

"Liar."

"It takes time for the pills to kick in."

"You need a new doctor."

"I'll think about it," Jill says.

I know she won't and no amount of talk is going to persuade her. I shovel in half my eggs and get up from the table.

"I'm off," I say. "Kiss Yvette for me."

"Joe." Jill grabs my arm as I start to walk away from the table. "If they haven't caught those maniacs by tonight, you come back here to sleep. I don't want you alone in your house while they're still on the loose."

I smile and lean down and kiss her in the forehead.

"Will do, my lovely," I say. "Thanks for the invitation."

And on that note, I walk out.

As I climb into my car, I check my watch. Ten minutes to eight. I'm positive the Academy doesn't open until nine at the earliest so I head for downtown, knowing that Mick will be at his desk. He gets to work at seven a.m. rain or shine. Miscreants need bail at all hours of the day and night.

Sure enough, he's in his office, huddled over a mountain of paperwork, a cold mug of coffee on one side and a cigarette burning in an ashtray on the other. He looks up with a smile when I appear in his doorway.

"That stuff'll kill you if you let it," I say.

"You're right," he says, stubbing out what's left of the cigarette butt. "I'm going to quit, starting tomorrow."

"I'm not talking about that. I mean all that paperwork under your nose."

"Gotta make a living, Joe," Mick says.

"That's the operative word, pal. Living. Bosses are supposed to let other people do the grunt work. Bosses are supposed to stay in bed late with their wives and have breakfast with their kids."

"You've been talking to Lydia." He sips his coffee.

"Don't have to. Ever wonder why there are so many rich widows around?"

He puts his coffee mug down and stares at me.

"Who put a bug up your butt this morning, Joe?"

"Nobody but if I had a wife like Lydia—"

"Which you once did—"

"Which I once did. I'd handle her like fragile crystal. You're a lucky guy, Mick. Don't take her for granted. Someone like her doesn't come along every day."

"I know and you're right," Mick says, leaning back in his chair.

"I'll be sixty next month, Joe. Lydia's not even forty yet. My oldest kid is eight. When he graduates high school and gets ready for college I'll be seventy if I live that long. I gotta make sure everybody's taken carc of."

"Sure, I get it, Mick, but the way I see it I think Lydia and the kids would rather have a few less bucks in the bank and a few more Christmases with you sitting around the tree."

"You're still young, Joe. You haven't reached the worry stage yet. Maybe you never will. You and Jill have more than enough to see Yvette gets well taken care of."

"And Bunny. Bunny, too, Mick."

He looks away without comment and then reaches in his pocket for his cigarettes.

"Maybe you know something I don't know," I say, suddenly afraid.

"I don't know anything, Joe," he says sharply. "Kim Patterson's still in Colorado. A glitch in the paperwork. I'll be lucky if he gets back by Saturday."

"So nobody's back east."

"That's right. Yesterday afternoon I made a few phone calls, Joe. I checked the flights out of Joplin for Ocala on that Friday and Saturday on the theory she was going to see him."

"And?"

"I drew a blank. She was on none of those flights. Then I checked all the flights out of Joplin headed anywhere. No Bunny. Wherever she went she could have taken the bus or the train, maybe even driven. It's a dead end until I can get Patterson out there with Bunny's picture to wave around and like I said, that would be Saturday at the earliest."

I'm disappointed but what can I do?

"Sure, Mick. I understand. What about this guy Kelso?"

"He was on a early Saturday flight to El Paso, Texas."

"And?"

"And nothing. That's all I know."

"But Bunny didn't fly to El Paso."

"I just told you that, Joe," Mick snaps at me.

I'm embarrassed. I'm acting like a jerk.

"Sorry, Mick," I say. "Whatever you can do. I appreciate it."

"No problem. Happy to do it," Mick says flatly as he turns his attention back to his paperwork.

"You think I'm crazy."

"I think you're hopeful," he says without looking up.

"There's an explanation."

"No doubt."

"I mean it," I say forcefully.

He looks up sharply from his paperwork and looks me in the eye. He's angry.

"Okay, you mean it. You may be a hundred per cent wrong but you mean it and you want me to go along except I don't go along. Much as I love you like a buddy, I'm not going to participate in your fantasies."

"No one asked you—"

"She's a runner, Joe, and she's running now, just like she ran away from you to go to New York and then from the magazine and then from the hospital in White Plains. It's what she does to avoid her demons. I've been in this business long enough to know there are demons, real ones, and everybody's are different. I'm sure she loves you, Joe. I'm sure deep down she wants to live happily ever after but she hasn't escaped from her own personal hell yet and until she does she'll always be in the wind. That's my speech. You have permission to punch me in the nose."

I stare at him silently. That couldn't have been easy for him. He thought it was something that had to be said and maybe he's right. Maybe I'm hoping desperately for something from Bunny that deep down she's unable to give. Maybe I can't face it, or won't face it, because I know I can't deal with the pain it's going to bring.

"Okay," I say.

"Okay, then," he says.

I move to the door.

"As soon as Patterson gets back, I'll send him right out to Joplin," Mick says.

I turn back to him.

"You're right," I say. "No sense to it."

"I'm sending him anyway. I could be dead wrong. You could be right. Lydia and I care about you, Joe. I think we need to know for sure and we need to know it now."

I nod.

"Call me when you've got something," I say and then walk out of the office.

I get back in my car and head for Wilshire Boulevard in Beverly Hills. I'm having trouble concentrating on my driving because my mind's tumbling erratically trying to get a grip on my conversation with Mick. He's a friend and the best kind, one who'll level with you even if it hurts. He didn't say anything to me that I haven't said to myself a hundred times. Am I about to embark on another fruitless search? How many weeks and months will have to pass before I face reality? I'm getting tired of eating alone and sleeping in an empty bed. Forty is close at hand. I don't want to live this way any longer. I can't.

I turn onto Wilshire and a few blocks later I pull into the parking lot of the Academy of Motion Picture Arts and Sciences. I park in a spot marked 'Visitors" and sit quietly for several minutes trying to work up the energy to walk inside. My early morning inspiration doesn't seem very important now. Avery Sterling and Joel Walberg are dead. Okay, so they're dead. It's really none of my business. I'm free and clear of this whole mess. Let the cops figure it out.

And then I remember Vito Ciello and realize I can't leave it to him so I get out of the car and walk inside. AMPAS is the Smithsonian of the movie industry, the keeper of the flame lit a century ago by the likes of Lasky and DeMille and Griffith. It's archives are massive and cover everything from photos to posters to well-preserved films and scripts and God knows what else going back decades. An attractive young lady, perhaps a budding actress, is at the information desk and when I tell her what I'm looking for, she directs me to the second floor. There I find another information desk and seated there is a face I recognize immediately.

"Good morning, Mr. Hopper," I say warmly.

He looks up at me in surprise and smiles.

"You know me?"

"Of course. Who could forget you?"

Fritz Hopper, born Hauptmann, spent WWII playing every nasty Nazi in existence from 1941 until 1946 when the public's taste for war movies started to wane. Two years later MGM came up with 'Battleground' and John Wayne was fighting on the sands of Iwo Jima but by then Fritz had converted himself into a cuddly European eccentric in dozens of comedies. He's older now, his hair white and thinning but there is no mistaking him. I reel off a half-dozen of his most famous roles. His eyes widen as does his grin.

"You honor me, young man," he says.

"Deservedly," I say.

"Danke scheon," he says. "And how may I help you?"

"I'm looking for a script. An award winner from 1938. I understand you have a copy."

He nods.

"We have most of them. Nominees and winners. The name, please."

"At Long Last, Farewell by Joel Walberg."

He reaches into his desk and takes out a large ledger and starts to leaf through it. I think I hear him humming 'Lili Marlene' but I can't be sure. It was the one picture that netted him a Supporting nomination.

"Yes. Here it is. I can let you read it on the premises but you may not remove it from the reading room."

"That's fine." I say.

He turns a large open Visitor's Register toward me.

"Sign please."

I take out a pen and do so, scanning the names above mine. I see nothing familiar but the register goes back only three days.

"Tell me, Mr. Hopper," I ask, "has anyone else inquired about this script in the last week or so?"

"Not that I remember," he says. "I will look."

Quickly he leafs through the preceding three pages and then shakes his head.

"No, nothing, Mr.—-" He checks my signature. "Mr. Bernardi." He gets up from his desk. "Come follow me."

He leads me to the reading room which is deserted at this hour of the morning, sits me down and disappears through a nearby door. Five minutes later he reappears carrying a manila envelope which he sets down in front of me. "I don't have to tell you to handle this with utmost care."

"No, you don't."

"When you are finished, bring it out to me at the desk."

"I will."

As he walks away I slip the unbound script out of the envelope. It is yellowing but highly readable. I don't need to read the script because I remember the film very well. I turn the script over and start looking through the last three or four pages until I find what I am looking for. I take a note pad and pen from my pocket and start copying. Ten minutes later I emerge from the reading room and drop the script on Fritz Hopper's desk. He looks up in amazement.

"You are a fast reader," he says.

"No, Mr. Hopper, just selective."

I wish him a good day and head back to my car. The cloud is starting to lift from this case. I think I am close but I'm not sure. I need to talk to Aaron.

CHAPTER NINETEEN

It's amazing how much you can get done in a day if you roll out of bed at six o'clock. I'm back at the office and it isn't even eleven o'clock. I ask Glenda Mae to get me Aaron. She buzzes me back. He's out of the office. She left word. I tell her I'm going to need to speak to Jack Warner and all the production heads at the major studios. She says she'll get right on it.

I hang up the intercom and start to look through my mail when she buzzes me. Fast worker, that girl.

"I got a cop out here wants to see you," she says.

"Ciello?"

"You mean the oil slick from the other day? No, this guy's name is Daryl Jenks."

Sure, the skinny little guy with the bad teeth.

"Send him in," I say.

A moment later, Jenks walks through the door. I rise to greet him. He points to the bandage on my forehead. It's been reduced from a giant white wad of gauze and cotton to a little butterfly.

"I heard about that. Somebody doesn't like you, Mr. Bernardi," Jenks says.

"Because they think I'm getting too close to the truth."

"And are you?"

"Where's your partner?" I say, ignoring his question, as I beckon him to a chair.

"Off the case," Jenks says.

"Really?" I can't believe my good luck. "How the hell did that happen?"

"They promoted him to Detective Third Grade,"

"Oh, Jesus. You're kidding."

"Nope. His uncle, the Deputy Chief, didn't much care what was being written about his nephew in the newspapers so he had him transferred to the CCSS."

"What's that?"

"Cold Case Special Section. Ciello's walking on air. Because he made Detective 3, he doesn't realize he's been kicked sideways into a black hole."

"So I guess that this means the Avery Sterling murder is all yours."

"You got it."

"Congratulations, Daryl. I'm relieved."

"You should be. And it's Duffy. Nobody calls me Daryl."

"Then you're not here to arrest me."

"No, and I also don't plan to extradite Welles from Timbuktoo or wherever he's staying these days."

"The Canary Islands, not that it matters," I say.

Jenks takes a small brown half-smoked cigarillo from his shirt pocket and lights up with a kitchen match that he strikes on the sole of his shoe.

"They found your prints at the scene of the Walberg suicide," he says.

"Pete Rodriguez knows all about that," I say.

"But I don't," Jenks says. "Enlighten me."

I tell him about my hour long kaffee klatch with Walberg. The room is beginning to smell like a barn.

"And you went to question him, why?"

'Well, let's see," I say, "Your dolt of a partner was looking to put me away in San Quentin for the rest of my natural life so I thought maybe I ought to poke around a little in self defense and when I realized that Walberg was working for Sterling under an assumed name, I thought a chat might be in order."

"And you learned what?"

"Not much. And what have you learned, Duffy?"

"About the same. I just took over this morning and Ciello didn't tell me much."

"I see. Well, let me get you up to speed. It's a pretty straightforward case. Ridiculously simple, in fact. You won't have any trouble sorting things out. Sterling's girlfriend, Pauline, who is married to Jamie, was screwing Sterling so she and her husband could get ahead in the business only Sterling was doublecrossing both of them by trying to get Orson Welles to direct this new movie instead of Jamie which made both of them more than a little irritable. And Walberg was pissed because Sterling was having his script rewritten by some penny-a-word hack and was ready to kill him which he didn't because the suicide thing is a clumsy set-up. Then there's Melinda McBride, the receptionist, who Sterling was also screwing, promising to get her big parts in major movies except the only thing he really got her was teed off enough to kill him. Not to mention Ralph Cacavas, the film editor who had been promised five thousand dollars by Sterling, money Cacavas needed for his ailing mother's medical expenses but Sterling reneged in paying him. And let's not forget Roy Watson who had been manhandling the books for almost a year which should look like a simple case of embezzlement but isn't. More on that in a minute. On the home front we have Henrietta Hanks, ex-hooker and old man Silver's live-in girl friend. Henrietta hated Sterling because he was squandering all the old man's money before she could get her hands on it. Douglas Webster, Jake Silver's right hand man, is the enforcer but he's much more than that. Secretly he's also Silver's son from a liaison in Chicago years ago with a hat check girl and he loved his legitimate brother the way Cain loved Abel. Next we have Oscar, the ex-wrestler with a plate in his head who is known to go berserk from time to time. And oh, yes, forgot to mention. Webster, Watson and Sterling were partners in a porno movie operation which was making a ton of money until Sterling wanted to get out of the skin flick business and make a legitimate movie, an idea that his partners despised in the extreme. Am I leaving anything out? I don't think so. There you have it, Duffy. Run with it."

Duffy stares at me, mouth agape.

"Jesus," he says quietly.

"This case has more suspects than Carter has liver pills. I feel like I'm in the middle of a Charlie Chan movie."

"Guess maybe I better start interviewing these people," Jenks says.

"Yeah, let 'em lie to YOU for a change."

"You got any thoughts on who did it?"Jenks asks.

"I might. I was going to discuss it with Aaron Kleinschmidt."

"Discuss it with me," Jenks says.

I shake my head.

"Don't know you well enough. Don't trust you, either. Not yet."

"How about if we both discuss it with Aaron?"Jenks suggests.

I think that over.

"Sure. Why not? Later today. I have a call in to him. I'll let you know what time."

Jenks stands up and extends his hand over my desk. I stand and we shake.

"Between the three of us, we're gonna get this son of a bitch, you just wait and see if we don't," Jenks says and then he turns and leaves, smoke from his little cigar wafting all around his head.

I am relieved that I'm no longer the object of police curiosity and equally happy for Orson who is undoubtedly stuffing himself on mojo picon at some cantina in Las Palmas and drinking massive amounts of malavania wine between courses.

Glenda Mac buzzes me. She has Jack Warner on the line. Well, that is not exactly true. Chances are she has Jack's secretary on the line. When I pick up, she will say, 'Please hold for Mr. Warner' and then Jack will come on the line. It's a little piece of Hollywood gamesmanship that Jack's been playing all his life just like the other moguls.

I pick up the phone.

"Hello."

"Please hold for Mr. Warner," comes this sweet voice. A moment later Jack is bellowing in my ear.

"Joe, how the hell are you?" he says.

"Fine," I tell him.

"I hear you've been consorting with Orson Welles. Watch yourself there, lad. Orson's a slick old con artist."

"I think you exaggerate, Jack."

"Not I. By the way, I loved that piece Phineas Ogilvy ran the other day about Orson's new picture and U-I's hamhanded editing. I told Curtiz you were behind that, am I right?"

"Well, Jack, I'm not one to give advice to a sage studio executive such as yourself but I saw Orson's first cut on this picture and if I were running a studio and I had a chance to buy the picture from a studio that was dissatisfied with it, I would do so without hesitation."

"That good?"

"That good," I say.

"I'll look into it," he says. "Now what's up, my friend. You didn't call to hype Welles' film. What's on your mind?"

I tell him and he replies that he has no idea what I am talking about. I take him at his word and after another couple of minutes I hang up.

I spend the rest of the afternoon doing make work, waiting to talk to the moguls. I keep striking out and I think that maybe I'm going with a bad hunch. Then at quarter to five I get Harry Cohn on the phone. Harry doesn't chit-chat a lot so he growls "Whatdayawant?" and I tell him and he says, "Yeah, that's right. What about it?" I don't feel like wasting any more time in frivolous conversation so I hang up. However, Harry has confirmed my hunch. Another piece fits in neatly. The fog is lifting. I'm close. I'm very close.

I buzz Glenda Mae.

"One last call, gorgeous, " I say. " Get me Duffy Jenks."

CHAPTER TWENTY

Friday morning. It's going to be a big day. The time is nine-thirty. By noon someone is going to be wearing a pair of handcuffs and be perp-walked to a waiting squad car. I'm scheduled to meet Duffy Jenks at Central Division Headquarters at ten sharp. We'll pick up Aaron at Parker Center and go together to make the arrest. The phone rings and a moment later Glenda Mae buzzes me. I pick up.

"Aaron," she says.

I punch the button for line one.

"Ready to go?" I ask.

"Sorry, Joe. It's on you and Duffy. A patrol car found a decapitated female in an alley behind a jewelry store on Rodeo Drive. On the theory that she may be someone with high up connections, it's all hands on deck. That means me."

"Duffy and I can handle it," I say.

"Sure you can. Keep me posted."

"Will do."

I hang up. It's not really a problem. I don't really expect armed resistance but if there is Duffy can deal with it. I tell Glenda Mae where I'm going and head out. We've already decided I would drive so as I swing up to the front entrance of Division headquarters,

Duffy's outside waiting for me. He hops in and we take off. A squad car pulls in behind us. This is our backup.

Twenty minutes later Duffy and I are walking up to the front door. I push the doorbell and hear the chime from within. No response. I try again. A moment later the door opens a few inches and a Chinese houseboy peers out. He could be Keye Luke's twin brother but he speaks English like I speak Bulgarian. Not here, go away, he tells us. When I become insistent he finally tells us, go to office. Do work, maybe. I try to get more out of him but he slams the door in our faces and no amount of finger power on the doorbell is going to get him to reappear.

We return to my car and I make a U-turn out of there. Next stop, the offices of Avery Sterling Productions. Traffic is light and it doesn't take long. I park at the curb. The squad car with the two uniforms pulls in behind us. Duffy tells them to wait and then he and I go inside the massive lobby and make a beeline for the elevators. I push the button for 3 and when the cab stops, we step out into the dimly lit corridor. It looks the same but even though the lights are on in the office suite there is an eerie quietness that I hadn't noticed before. A double murderer is skulking about these offices, a killer without a conscience who would blow me away without a second thought. I'm glad Duffy is with me and I'm doubly glad he is armed.

I push through the double doors with Duffy right behind me. I stop, standing stock still, listening for signs of life. Now I hear them. Muffled voices. But from where? I'm not sure. All of the office doors are closed. I go to one nearby and peer in. Empty. I try the next and the next. All vacant but the sound of voices grows louder. Acrimony. Anger. Something's going on. I head toward the door to the conference room at the end of the corridor, open it and peer in. Nine faces whip around and stare at me. We have interrupted some sort of meeting.

At the head of the table sits Jake Silver, elegantly dressed in a three piece grey flannel suit. Flanking him are Douglas Webster and Henny Hanks. Henny is startled. Webster looks malevolent. Next to Webster sits Pauline Kreitzmann and across from her is her husband Jamie wearing his ever present white carnation boutonniere. Next to Jamie is Roy Watson who regards me as he always does, with a superior sneer on his face. Ralph Cacavas is seated next to Pauline and facing Ralph is Melanie McBride who has a notepad in front of her and seems to be acting as secretary for the proceedings. Oscar is also on hand, sitting by himself on a chair next to the wall.

I step into the room followed closely by Duffy. Jake Silver glares at me.

"This is a private meeting, Mr. Bernardi," he says. "You don't belong here."

"You're wrong, Mr. Silver. I am in exactly the right place, that is, if you are the least bit interested in learning who killed your son."

That gets a reaction. Ralph Cacavas shakes his head slightly and looks away. Henny looks at Douglas Webster who looks down the table at Roy Watson. Watson looks sharply toward Pauline who wrinkles her brow as she glances toward her husband.

"I'll handle this, Mr. Silver," Webster says angrily as he starts to get to his feet. The old man grabs his sleeve and yanks at him.

"Sit down, Douglas," he says as he keeps his gaze fixated on me. "And the gentleman with you? The police?"

"Detective Daryl Jenks," I say. I feel very uncomfortable. Duffy and I had planned to walk in, grab the perp and walk out without fuss or bother. Now it seems we've walked into a UN security council meeting and there is no way to do this elegantly.

"I didn't kill him!"

I'm startled as an hysterical Ralph Cacavas gets to his feet, his face white and sweaty, his eyes red and fearful.

"I know it's my fingerprints they found in the office but I didn't kill him, I just wanted my money, that's all. My Mom was dying in that hospital. I couldn't let it happen. I was just working the combination on the safe when he walked in."

I look over at Duffy. This is something new. He looks back at me, as puzzled as I am.

"Anyway, it wasn't much of a fight." Cacavas says. "I swung at him hard and lost my balance and then when I was on the floor, he kicked me twice. I scrambled toward the door and ran for it. But I swear on my mother's life, he was alive when I left."

"No one's accusing you, Mr. Cacavas—-" I say but I'm interrupted by Jake Silver.

"And where the hell did you get the combination to the safe?" he demands to know.

"Never mind!" Cacavas shouts at him.

"I gave it to him."

All eyes turn to Melanie McBride.

"I visited Ralph's mother three times," she says. "It was a terrible sight. She was so thin and frail and nobody was doing anything for her. I knew it was up to me to help."

"You're fired, young lady!" Jake shouts from the head of the table.

"Fired from what?" Roy Watson says loudly. "This company's dead. Everybody knows it."

"Excuse me," I say trying to get a word in.

"You're wrong, Watson," says Jamie Kreitzmann. "Unless you've stolen all the money, this company still has a very valuable asset in Joel Walberg's final script which I intend to direct."

Henny Hanks pipes up.

"Joel Walberg was a Commie son of a bitch and that screenplay is unproducible—"

"Says who?" Jamie shouts.

"Says the damned government," Henny responds. "His name's on the blacklist and besides, nobody is spending another dime of Jakey-poo's money on this goddamned company."

Jakey-poo? Jake Silver may be a lot of things, but a Jakey-poo he is not. I try again to regain control of the room.

"Folks, if I could just have your attention—"

"Don't you mean YOUR money, Henrietta," Pauline chimes in. "If I were you, Jake, I'd hire myself a taster because if she knocked off Avery, she won't have any qualms about putting you away."

"Speak for yourself, bitch," Henny responds. "My guess is Avery got tired of you and you iced him while the icing was good."

"I resent that slur on my wife's good name," Jamie says angrily.

"Good name? When did that start?" Roy Watson chimes in.

"What right have you got to say that?" Melanie says loudly, "You and your dirty movies."

"Dirty movies? What dirty movies?" Jake Silver asks, bewildered.

"And you're the biggest whore of all, Miss McBride," says Douglas Webster, "spreading your legs to get a part in a movie and when you don't get one, you threaten to commit murder."

"I didn't—-"

"You did. Nine days ago in the clothes closet. I heard you. Everybody heard you,"

"I didn't mean it! I was just blowing off steam."

"That's not all you were blowing, kiddo," Roy Watson says snidely.

"Of course she didn't mean it," Pauline chimes in. "Isn't it obvious who the killer is? The bastard son who's gotten nothing while the profligate legitimate son gets everything. Jealousy and hatred. There's your motive."

I look over at Duffy who is standing nearby, arms folded, surveying the scene with a jaundiced eye. He looks as if he'd like to shoot the lot of them.

"Quiet!" I shout. It has no effect. I feel helpless. Hercule Poirot, the consummate know-it-all, never undergoes this sort of indignity when he tries to reveal the name of the killer. I've watched dozens of Perry Masons and Raymond Burr doesn't have to contend with acrimonious backbiting by his suspects. Maybe because he's in a courtroom there's a bit more decorum. I don't know. All I know is I have something to say and I can't get a chance to say it. Duffy sees my distress and takes charge.

"Hey!" he shouts as loud as he can. "You people! Shut the hell up!"

All eyes turn toward Duffy and me. The silence in the room is deafening. For the briefest of moments we are a frozen tableau. Then I speak.

"Now that I have your attention, I will identify the killer and after that you may go on with your meeting." I slowly look around the room, pausing for effect. "Shortly after the body was discovered by the janitor, the police were notified and within an hour a forensics team was on site gathering evidence. As you know only two sets of fingerprints were discovered, one being Avery Sterling's and the other belonging to Ralph Cacavas. Mr. Cacavas freely admits he was there that night and was severely beaten by Mr. Sterling.

"I wouldn't say severely," Cacavas chimes in.

"Yes, yes, we know all that," Jake Silver says. "Can we get on with it?"

"The police also found five clues, each of which pointed to one of you as the killer. For instance a pair of black framed eyeglasses belonging to Oscar Trippi."

"I told you, I lost those," Oscar shouts from his chair against the wall.

"Relax, Oscar," I say. "You didn't kill anybody. And then there was a woman's gold earring. Gold with a diamond."

"Like the kind you wear, Henrietta," Douglas Webster says nastily.

"Go to hell, you bastard," she says.

"But the earring didn't belong to Henrietta because it was a clip on and Henrietta only wears earrings for her pierced ears."

All eyes turn to Melanie McBride.

"Nor was it Melanie who never would have shot Avery because she has a pathological fear of guns."

Now all eyes turn to Pauline,

"Nor did the earring belong to Pauline Kreitzmann because Pauline wears her hair long and straight, covering her ears. A woman whose ears are constantly covered does not wear earrings."

"Then who—" Melanie starts to say.

"Nobody," I say.

"Hey!" Jake Silver yells. "What kind of bullshit is this? This one didn't do it, that one didn't do it. You want to show off,mister, get a job with the circus."

"The clues were plants, Mr. Silver. Like the petals from a white carnation and the bloody monogrammed handkerchief, all left at the scene in order to confuse and befuddle the police."

"Yeah, yeah, but get to the point," Jake says. "You're wasting our time."

"I'm getting to the point," I say, "if you'll just have a little patience."

"I'm trying, Mr. Bernardi, but I've got a lunch date at noon," says Roy Watson.

"And I have an appointment with my hairdresser," Henny Hanks says.

"Get on with it, Bernardi," says Jamie Kreitzmann. "This is getting boring."

Again I think, something is wrong. Charlie Chan and Nero Wolfe never had to put up with this kind of rudeness. The suspects would sit quietly while Charlie and Nero preened and bloviated, never daring to interrupt the master detectives. I'm doing this wrong, I think to myself.

"The planted clues weren't working. That's why Joel Walberg

was murdered," I say.

"He wasn't murdered, he committed suicide," Ralph Cacavas says, now calmed to the point that he is coherent.

"No, it was murder, Ralph. The killer had to do away with him. He needed Walberg's suicide to close the case before the police got too close to the truth. And because I was adamant that the suicide had been staged and because at least one higher up in homicide was starting to believe me, an attempt was made to silence me. On Wednesday night I was shot at and run off the road. Luckily I survived."

"Who? Who tried to kill you?" the old man says impatiently. "Was it that gonef down at the end of the table?"

"Hey, I didn't kill him." Roy Watson says defensively.

"No, you didn't, Mr. Watson, " I say. "You had no reason. You were making enough money that Avery could no longer help you or hurt you. With all the money you had salted away, he was basically irrelevant."

Jake Silver throws up his hands in frustration.

"Wonderful! Another one who didn't do it."

"It had to do with the suicide note," I say. "Word for word, it had been lifted from Joel Walberg's most famous movie script, 'At Long Last, Farewell'. At the end, an English barrister who has committed murder goes to his typewriter and types out a suicide note, a farewell to the world that has treated him badly and when he has finished he takes out a pistol and blows his brains out."

"Okay, so Walberg got a little theatrical and borrowed from one of his old scripts," Roy Watson says.

"Not so, Mr. Watson. Joel told me very emphatically that he wrote 'em and forgot 'em. And even if he had somehow remembered the note after all these years, he never would have spelled 'honour' with a 'u'. The barrister in the movie was English. Joel Walberg was not. And finally, Joel told me that he hated the many creaky melodramatic plot moves in the script and what more creaky than this melodramatic suicide. No, this note was typed by a man who remembered that film all too well, a man with a photographic memory who forgets nothing about the movies he sees, a man who was offered a directorial assignment by Harry Cohn at Columbia Pictures, a job he was forced to turn down because Avery Sterling would not release him from his personal services contract even as Avery was trying to replace him as director—"

"All right!" Jamie Kreitzmann screams, leaping to his feet. He stands for a moment, shuddering, his face contorted in pain. "All right," he continues more quietly. "Yes, I killed him. He deserved to die. He was an animal without conscience, a man without integrity who used and abused people without a second thought and then tossed them away like used Kleenex."

Douglas Webster leans toward him.

"Be quiet, Jamie. They have no real proof. A good lawyer can get you off."

"I know, I know," he says. "But I just can't hold it in any longer. He was such a shit, the world's a better place without him."

"Jamie, there's a police officer standing over there taking all of this in," Webster says. "Just stop talking."

"He was just so evil, so rotten to the core."

"Will you just shut up!" Webster shouts at him. "F. Lee Bailey is available!"

"He cared nothing for anyone other than himself," Jamie continues. "I actually felt a thrill putting that bullet between his eyes."

His wife, Pauline, reaches across the table and gently takes his hand. "My darling, I can hardly believe this but I am going to stand by you no matter what."

"You bet you will, princess," I say, "you will be standing right beside him, at the arraignment and at the trial when you are jointly tried for murder."

She glares at me.

"Ridiculous!"

"Maybe to you," I say. "but I'm pretty sure you fired the first shot, the one to Avery's private parts. That was the act of a woman used and betrayed, and when you had finished pulling the trigger I think you handed the gun to your husband to inflict the coup de grace. I think it was you in the back seat of the car the other night, the one who fired the gun at me. And even more than that, I think that Avery Sterling's murder was really your idea."

She looks at me and then turns her head away. Silence falls over the table. There is not a lot left to say. Duffy sidles over to me and speaks quietly out of the side of his mouth.

"You should have warned me about the woman," he says.

"Sorry," I say. "Is there a problem?"

He nods solemnly.

"I only brought one set of cuffs."

CHAPTER TWENTY-ONE

I'm exhausted. The last ten days have wrung me dry. I never want to hear or see the name Sterling again, not even on my silverware. Even though it's over I still have a headache, the same one I got trying to sort out the red herrings from the real deals. I'm driving Duffy back to Central Division and he is watching me closely, wondering if I'm all right. I assure him that I am but I don't think he believes me. The two uniforms have gone on ahead with Jamie and Pauline to start the booking process. The others remained behind to finish their meeting and something tells me it was all about the thriving porno business which they all now want a piece of. I could be wrong but I don't think so.

I drop Duffy off. We shake hands. He's sharp and he's honest and more importantly, Aaron likes him. It won't be long before he makes Sergeant. I drive off and head back to the office. It's nearly noon and I think I'll invite Bertha to lunch. We haven't touched base in days and we need to catch up. I also owe a few phone calls, especially one to Orson who needs to be reassured that the LAPD is not going to be trying to extradite him any time soon.

Glenda Mae has a phone number for a banana plantation near Las Palmas in the Canary Islands where Orson and Noel Coward have been staying as guests of the owner, a Senor Valdez. It is to

Valdez that I am speaking after Glenda Mae has me connected. He is sorry but Mr. Welles and Mr. Coward are no longer visiting him. Mr. Coward has returned to the Bahamas and Mr. Welles has flown to Africa where he is filming a movie in Chad with Errol Flynn. No, he has left no forwarding address or phone number. I hang up, resigned to the fact that it might be weeks or months before I once again hear from my gadabout friend. Orson Welles, world traveler, free spirit, and one man band. There is no one else like him.

I phone Aaron to tell him the good news but he's already heard it from Duffy. He thinks I am a lucky son of a bitch but glad I am still alive. I thank him for his critique and get ready to walk down the corridor to Bertha's office when Glenda Mae buzzes me. I pick up.

"His name is Costa. He's with the Highway Patrol. He wouldn't say what it was about but his tone wasn't cheerful."

I feel a chill run down my back as I punch the lit button on my phone.

"This is Joe Bernardi," I say.

"Mr. Bernardi, this is Lt. Costa with the California Highway Patrol. Are you acquainted with an Elizabeth Lesher?"

Bunny. Oh, God, I think as my mouth turns dry.

"Yes, I am, " I manage to say.

"There was an accident earlier this morning. A nine-car pile up in the fog on Interstate 5 near Valencia. We found your name and number in her wallet as her emergency contact."

"Is she all right?" I ask. What I mean is, is she alive?

"She's been taken to Olive View Hospital in Sylmar for treatment. Beyond that I have no information."

I thank him for notifying me and hang up. I head out, stopping only to tell Glenda Mae where I am going and that I am unreachable for the foreseeable future. Within minutes I'm on the road headed for Sylmar.

A thousand thoughts are running through my mind as I drive

north on Interstate 5. What was Bunny doing driving the freeway earlier this morning? Was she alone? Costa made no mention of a passenger. Maybe that was an oversight. I have no idea of her condition. Maybe Costa didn't know. Maybe Costa didn't want to tell me.

I pull into the hospital parking lot and find a spot close to the main entrance. I hurry inside to the information desk where the volunteer looks up Bunny's name. Yes, she's been admitted but visiting hours don't begin until two o'clock. I lie and tell her that I am her husband. She tells me to check with the nurse's station on the second floor. I hurry to the elevator.

The head nurse is named B. Prohaska and I learn that the B stands for Beatrice. I also learn that Beatrice is smart, efficient and rule-conscious. No, I may not visit. Doctor's orders. But I also learn that she has a wide streak of humanity. She can't give me any patient information but she does get on the intercom and pages Bunny's doctor.

Fifteen minutes later I'm sitting in the waiting room when a youngish looking man in scrubs peers in the doorway.

"Mr. Bernardi?"

I get to my feet as he enters.

"I'm Doctor Bascomb." He puts out his hand. We shake. "I know you must be worried but I think your wife's going to get through this just fine. She suffered a lot of cuts and bruises as well as a minor concussion which we are monitoring but there are no broken bones and only minimum blood loss. She's really a very lucky woman."

"This is really good to hear, Doc," I say. "You have no idea."

He smiles. "Not being married myself, you're probably right."

Forget married, I'm not sure he's old enough to vote.

"I understand you'd like to visit her but at the moment she's asleep and I don't want her disturbed. Unless there are complications, which I don't expect, I think it will be possible for you to see her around suppertime."

I nod, thanking him and after he leaves, I head for the hospital cafeteria. Not that I'm hungry because I'm not, but I know I have to eat. I wolf down a bowl of turkey noodle soup and then go in search of a phone. I call Glenda Mae and tell her what's happened and ask her to pass it on to Bertha. Then I call Mick.

"Tell Kim Patterson to take the weekend off," I say.

"Why? What happened?"

I tell him.

"Sounds to me like Bunny's a very lucky lady," Mick says.

"Luckier than the three they brought in who didn't make it," I say.

"It also sounds like she was on her way home, Joe."

"Maybe so, Mick."

"No maybe about it. I was wrong, Joe, and I'm really glad I was. I'm sure Lydia will be pleased."

"I know she will. I'll probably hang around here until I can take Bunny home. Might be a day, maybe two or three. I have no idea."

"Okay. Keep in touch. We're thinking about you, buddy."

It takes me fifteen minutes to find a nearby Holiday Inn. Another fifteen minutes to locate a drug store where I buy a toothbrush, toothpaste, a razor, underwear and a pair of socks. I also pick up Ed McBain's latest book, "Killer's Choice". By two-thirty I'm back in the waiting room, this time in the company of a young Hispanic couple worried about her mother and a chubby oldster who keeps nodding off, only to be awakened by his own snoring.

With one eye on the clock I try to get into Ed McBain but by five thirty I've gotten only as far as page 4 and I can't remember what the book is about. Is Bunny really back in my life? Is that too much to hope for? Why didn't she tell me she was coming? Was she not planning to see me? A dozen painful questions I'd rather not deal with keep popping into my head and Ed McBain is no antidote.

I look up as Nurse Beatrice walks into the room. She beckons to me.

"She's awake," she says.

Bunny has never looked so awful or so beautiful. A bandage is wrapped around her head and I suspect they've had to shear off some of her beautiful hair to treat her. One of her cheeks sports a large white gauze bandage and her left eye is blackened and slightly swollen. She is resting peacefully and her eyes are closed as I step into the room. I think she senses my presence because she opens her eyes and looks up at me and breaks into a gorgeous smile.

"Surprise!" she says, feebly.

"You can say that again," I say.

"Surprise!" she echoes, just as feebly.

I walk over to the bed and sit on the edge and take her good hand in mine and hold it. She has an IV needle in the other one, pumping her full of fluids.

"Glad to see me?" she asks.

"You know I am," I tell her.

"This is absolutely fucking wrong, you know. I was supposed to be in the house before you got home. I'd have a turkey roasting in the oven and the table set with candles and Sinatra playing on the phonograph and instead I plow into the rear end of this stupid son of a bitch in a Volkswagen who has stopped dead in front of me."

"Because he had plowed into the car in front of him. Nine cars, Bunny. Five dead and one in a coma. You are one lucky lady."

"I am, I am and I'm grateful but this isn't the way I wanted it to be."

"I know."

"Maybe I should have called you," she says. "I almost did but then I decided it would be more fun to surprise you."

"Well, you always did like surprises. So how do you feel?"

"Not too bad, but they have me doped up."

"Tell me about James Kelso," I say.

"Jimmy? He stopped off at El Paso to see his mother. He said he was going to spend two or three days before coming to L.A."

"I mean, who is he? What's going on?"

"He used to work for the Globe before he got the job working for the Ocala paper."

"So I was told. A good friend?"

"The best. He didn't like it in Florida, not at all, and when the Valley News offered him the job of Editor, he jumped at it."

"You mean the Valley News here in the San Fernando Valley?"

"Yep, and the first thing he did was call me in Joplin and offer me a job as assistant editor. That's when I knew I was ready, Joe. It was a sign. I didn't think twice. I said yes."

"And does Jimmy know about me?" I ask.

"Of course he does," she says. She hesitates, looking into my eyes and then she smiles. "Oh, no. No, Joe, absolutely not. You don't know Jimmy. He's going on 50 and kind of gawky like a scarecrow with scraggly hair he cuts himself and has the sweetest disposition of anyone I know. He collects little tin soldiers from every war since the Revolution and stages mock battles in his basement. In good weather he goes out bird watching with a camera and has several dozen scrap books filled with his photos. He eats one meal a day, no meat and the food is grown organically. I love him to death like the big brother I never had."

I smile. "Then you two aren't secretly married?"

"Not that I recall. You'll like him, Joe. I know you will."

"I think you're probably right," I say. I squeeze her hand. "You look wonderful."

"Oh, sure. Me all decked out in Johnson & Johnson."

"Still going to meetings?" I ask.

"Every morning. Seven o'clock. Never miss. Going on three years, Joe. Doesn't mean I'm cured but it's a great start."

"We need to celebrate."

"Ready when you are," she says. "How's Yvette?"

"Wonderful. Has a little cold. She's milking the hell out of it. She's looking forward to meeting you."

Bunny's brow furrows. "You told her about me."

"I didn't. Jill did. A couple of months ago Yvette asked Jill why she didn't marry Uncle Joe so she could have a Daddy just like the other girls. Jill told her I was already married to Aunt Bunny and that she was a very lucky girl to have not only an Uncle Joe but a wonderful Aunt Bunny as well. Then she asked where you were and Jill said you would be coming home very soon. You are coming home, aren't you, Bunny?"

"Yes, Joe. I'm coming home. All the way if that's the way you want it."

"You know I do," I say.

"I'm not afraid any more, Joe. I'm tougher now. I can handle just about anything."

"I know you can."

"Hold me close, Joe," she says.

I lean forward and slip my arms behind her back and lay my head on her shoulder, feeling the warmth of her and taking in her sweet smell.

Bunny is home for good and I am content.

The End

AUTHOR'S NOTE

As a mystery buff, I love the stylized mechanics of the drawing room mysteries of an era that pre-dates WWII. Poirot was one of my earliest delights with his fussing and preening as he gathered his seven or eight likely suspects together and proceeded to waste at least a half hour until he finally relented and named the killer. Whether it was in the parlor car of a snowbound train or aboard an excursion boat steaming up the Nile. Poirot commanded attention and his creator, Miss Agatha Christie, demanded respect for the way she constructed the funny little Belgian's adventures. So it was out of love for the genre that I wrote this twelfth novel chronicling Joe Bernardi's travails in Hollywood. The convoluted plot involving Avery Sterling and those who despised him is rank nonsense. I can truly say about these people that any resemblance to persons living or dead is purely coincidental. However, Orson Welles' troubles with the editing and subsequent release of "Touch of Evil" are very real and except for a few grace notes here and there Welles' frustrations are accurately described in these pages. The 58 page memo outlining his suggestions for re-editing the picture was ignored by Universal- International and the film was released in February 1958 without fanfare and minimal advertising. It failed at the box office in the United States and the critics were divided in their opinion. Some called it brilliant, others thought it "artsy" and self-indulgent. Europe thought differently. Business was excellent and the film was named Best International Film at the World's Fair in Brussels. Nevertheless Welles never again directed in the U.S. for a major studio. In 1998, Walter Murch, one of the industry's finest editors, undertook to re-edit "Touch of Evil" by scrupulously following Welles' notes in the by-now famous 58 page memo. The results were widely hailed and even today, "Touch of Evil" is considered one of the major milestones in Orson Welles' storied career.

ABOUT THE AUTHOR

Peter S. Fischer is a former television writer-producer who currently lives with his wife Lucille in the Monterey Bay area of Central California. He is a co-creator of "Murder, She Wrote" for which he wrote over 40 scripts. Among his other credits are a dozen "Columbo" episodes and a season helming "Ellery Queen." He has also written and produced several TV mini-series and Movies of the Week. In 1985 he was awarded an Edgar by the Mystery Writers of America. In addition to four EMMY nominations, two Golden Globe Awards for Best TV series, and an Anthony Award from the Boucheron, he has received the IBPA award for the Best Mystery Novel of the Year, a Bronze Medal from the Independent Publishers Association and an Honorable Mention from the San Francisco Festival for his first novel.

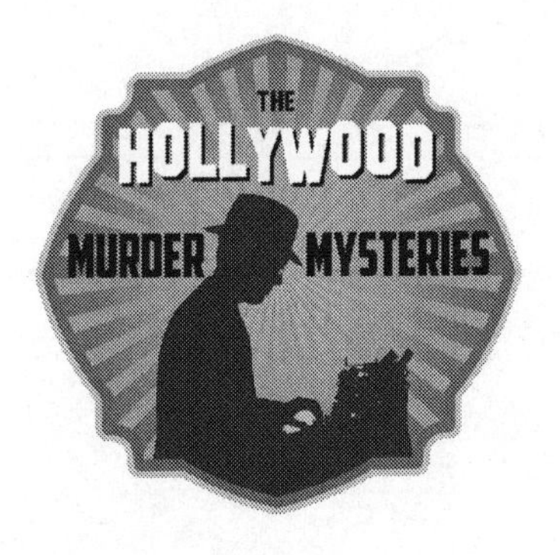
THE
HOLLYWOOD
MURDER
MYSTERIES

PRAISE FOR THE HOLLYWOOD MURDER MYSTERIES

Jezebel in Blue Satin

his stylish homage to the detective novels of Hollywood's Golden Age, a ss agent stumbles across a starlet's dead body and into the seamy world of eming players and morally bankrupt movie moguls.....An enjoyable fast- ed whodunit from opening act to final curtain.

—Kirkus Reviews

s of golden era Hollywood, snappy patter and Raymond Chandler will much to like in Peter Fischer's murder mystery series, all centered on school studio flak, Joe Bernardi, a happy-go-lucky war veteran who ls himself immersed in tough situations.....The series fills a niche that's n superseded by explosions and violence in too much of popular culture even though jt's a world where men are men and women are dames, its ıpses at an era where the facade of glamour and sophistication hid an er truth are still fun to revisit.

—2012 San Francisco Book Festival, Honorable Mention

bel in Blue Satin, set in 1947, finds movie studio publicist Joe Bernardi ıming it at a third rate motion picture house running on large egos and talent. When the ingenue from the film referenced in the title winds up d, can Joe uncover the killer before he loses his own life? Fischer makes an rtless transition from TV mystery to page turner, breathing new life into film noir hard boiled detective tropes. Although not a professional sleuth, s evolution from everyman into amateur private eye makes sense; any bad licity can cost him his job so he has to get to the bottom of things.

—ForeWord Review

We Don't Need No Stinking Badges

A thrilling mystery packed with Hollywood glamour, intrigue and murder, s in 1948 Mexico.....Although the story features many famous faces (Humph Bogart, director John Huston, actor Walter Huston and novelist B. Traven, to name a few), the plot smartly focuses on those behind the scenes. The big names aren't used as gimmicks—they're merely planets for the story to rota around. Joe Bernardi is the star of the show and this fictional tale in a real life setting (the actual set of 'Treasure of the Sierra Madre' was also fraught with problems) works well in Fischer's sure hands....A smart clever Mexica mystery.

—Kirkus Reviews

A former TV writer continues his old-time Hollywood mystery series, seamlessly interweaving fact and fiction in this drama that goes beyond the genre's cliches. "We Don't Need No Stinking Badges" again transports rea to post WWII Tinseltown inhabited by cinema publicist Joe Bernardi... Str characterization propels this book. Toward the end the crosses and double-crosses become confusing, as seemingly inconsequential things such as a de woman who was only mentioned in passing in the beginning now become matters on which the whole plot turns (but) such minor hiccups should not deter mystery lovers, Hollywood buffs or anyone who adores a good yarn.

—ForeWord Review

Peter S. Fischer has done it again—he has put me in a time machine and landed me in 1948. He has written a fast paced murder mystery that will h you up into the wee hours reading. If you love old movies, then this is the book for you.

—My Shelf. Com

This is a complex, well-crafted whodunit all on its own. There's plenty of action and adventure woven around the mystery and the characters are ful fashioned. The addition of the period piece of the 1940's filmmaking and inclusion of big name stars as supporting characters is the whipped cream cherry on top. It all comes together to make an engaging and fun read.

—Nyssa, Amazon Customer Review

Love Has Nothing to Do With It

:her's experience shows in 'Love Has Nothing To Do With It', an homage ilm noir and the hard-boiled detective novel. The story is complicated... but :her never loses the thread. The story is intricate enough to be intriguing not baffling....Joe Bernardi's swagger is authentic and entertaining. Overall 's a likable sleuth with the dogged determination to uncover the truth.... ile the outcome of the murder is an unknown until the final pages of the rent title, we do know that Joe Bernardi will survive at least until 1950, en further adventures await him in the forthcoming 'Everybody Wants an :ar'.

—Clarion Review

tylized, suspenseful Hollywood whodunit set in 1949....Goes down smooth murder-mystery fans and Old Hollywood junkies.

—Kirkus Review

Hollywood Murder Mysteries just might make a great Hallmark series. 's give this book: The envelope please: FIVE GOLDEN OSCARS.

—Samfreene, Amazon Customer Review

writing is fantastic and, for me, the topic was a true escape into our past rtainment world. Expect it to be quite different from today's! But that's readers will enjoy visiting Hollywood as it was in the past. A marvelous cept that hopefully will continue up into the 60s and beyond. Loved it!

—GABixlerReviews

The Unkindness of Strangers

Winner of the Benjamin Franklin Award
for Best Mystery Book of 2012
by the Independent Book Publisher's Association.

Book One—1947
JEZEBEL IN BLUE SATIN

WWII is over and Joe Bernardi has just returned home after three years as a war correspondent in Europe. Married in the heat of passion three weeks before he shipped out, he has come home to find his wife Lydia a complete stranger. It's not long before Lydia is off to Reno for a quickie divorce which Joe won't accept. Meanwhile he's been hired as a publicist by third rate movie studio, Continental Pictures. One night he enters a darkened sound stage only to discover the dead body of ambitious, would-be actress Maggie Baumann. When the police investigate, they immediately zero in on Joe as the perp. Short on evidence they attempt to frame him and almost succeed. Who really killed Maggie? Was it the over-the-hill actress trying for a comeback? Or the talentless director with delusions of grandeur? Or maybe it was the hapless leading man whose career is headed nowhere now that the "real stars" are coming back from the war. There is no shortage of suspects as the story speeds along to its exciting and unexpected conclusion.

Book Two—1948
WE DON'T NEED NO STINKING BADGES

Joe Bernardi is the new guy in Warner Brothers' Press Department so it's no surprise when Joe is given the unenviable task of flying to Tampico, Mexico, to bail Humphrey Bogart out of jail without the world learning about it. When he arrives he discovers that Bogie isn't the problem. So-called accidents are occurring daily on

Available in paperback or Kindle editions from Amazon.com

the set, slowing down the filming of "The Treasure of the Sierra Madre" and putting tempers on edge. Everyone knows who's behind the sabotage. It's the local Jefe who has a finger in every illegal pie. But suddenly the intrigue widens and the murder of one of the actors throws the company into turmoil. Day by day, Joe finds himself drawn into a dangerous web of deceit, dupliciity and blackmail that nearly costs him his life.

Book Three—1949
LOVE HAS NOTHING TO DO WITH IT

Joe Bernardi's ex-wife Lydia is in big, big trouble. On a Sunday evening around midnight she is seen running from the plush offices of her one- time lover, Tyler Banks. She disappears into the night leaving Banks behind, dead on the carpet with a bullet in his head. Convinced that she is innocent, Joe enlists the help of his pal, lawyer Ray Giordano, and bail bondsman Mick Clausen, to prove Lydia's innocence, even as his assignment to publicize Jimmy Cagney's comeback movie for Warner's threatens to take up all of his time. Who really pulled the trigger that night? Was it the millionaire whose influence reached into City Hall? Or the not so grieving widow finally freed from a loveless marriage. Maybe it was the partner who wanted the business all to himself as well as the new widow. And what about the mysterious envelope, the one that disappeared and everyone claims never existed? Is it the key to the killer's identity and what is the secret that has been kept hidden for the past forty years?

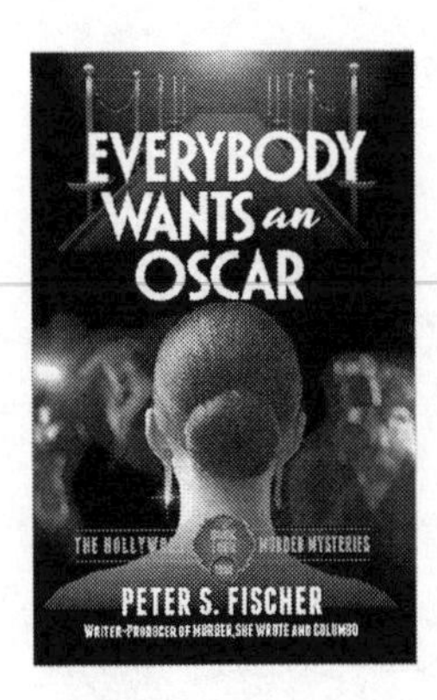

Book Four—1950
EVERYBODY WANTS AN OSCAR

After six long years Joe Bernardi's novel is at last finished and has been shipped to a publisher. But even as he awaits news, fingers crossed for luck, things are heating up at the studio. Soon production will begin on Tennessee Williams' "The Glass Menagerie" and Jane Wyman has her sights set on a second consecutive Academy Award. Jack Warner has just signed Gertrude Lawrence for the pivotal role of Amanda and is positive that the Oscar will go to Gertie. And meanwhile Eleanor Parker, who has gotten rave reviews for a prison picture called "Caged" is sure that 1950 is her year to take home the trophy. Faced with three very talented ladies all vying for his best efforts, Joe is resigned to performing a monumental juggling act. Thank God he has nothing else to worry about or at least that was the case until his agent informed him that a screenplay is floating around Hollywood that is a dead ringer for his newly completed novel. Will the ladies be forced to take a back seat as Joe goes after the thief that has stolen his work, his good name and six years of his life?

Book Five—1951
THE UNKINDNESS OF STRANGERS

Warner Brothers is getting it from all sides and Joe Bernardi seems to be everybody's favorite target. "A Streetcar Named Desire" is unproducible, they say. Too violent, too seedy, too sexy, too controversial and what's worse, it's being directed by that well-known pinko, Elia Kazan. To make matters worse, the country's number one hate monger, newspaper columnist Bryce Tremayne, is coming after Kazan with a vengeance and nothing Joe can do or say will stop him. A vicious expose column is set to run in every Hearst paper in the nation on the upcoming Sunday but a funny thing happens Friday night. Tremayne is found in a compromising condition behind the wheel of his car, a bullet hole between his eyes. Come Sunday and the scurrilous attack on Kazan does not appear. Rumors fly. Kazan is suspected but he's not the only one with a motive. Consider:

Elvira Tremayne, the unloved widow. Did Tremayne slug her one time too many?

Hubbell Cox, the flunky whose homosexuality made him a target of derision.

Willie Babbitt, the muscle. He does what he's told and what he's told to do is often unpleasant.

Jenny Coughlin, Tremayne's private secretary. But how private and what was her secret agenda?

Jed Tompkins, Elvira's father, a rich Texas cattle baron who had only contempt for his son-in-law.

Boyd Larabee, the bookkeeper, hired by Tompkins to win Cox's confidence and report back anything he's learned.

Annie Petrakis, studio makeup artist. Tremayne destroyed her lover. Has she returned the favor?

Book Six—1952
NICE GUYS FINISH DEAD

Ned Sharkey is a fugitive from mob revenge. For six years he's been successfully hiding out in the Los Angeles area while a $100, 000 contract for his demise hangs over his head. But when Warner Brothers begins filming "The Winning Team", the story of Grover Cleveland Alexander, Ned can't resist showing up at the ballpark to reunite with his old pals from the Chicago Cubs of the early 40's who have cameo roles in the film. Big mistake. When Joe Bernardi, Warner Brothers publicity guy, inadvertently sends a press release and a photo of Ned to the Chicago papers, mysterious people from the Windy City suddenly appear and a day later at break of dawn, Ned's body is found sprawled atop the pitcher's mound. It appears that someone is a hundred thousand dollars richer. Or maybe not. Who is the 22 year old kid posing as a 50 year old former hockey star? And what about Gordo Gagliano, a mountain of a man, who is out to find Ned no matter who he has to hurt to succeed? And why did baggy pants comic Fats McCoy jump Ned and try to kill him in the pool parlor? It sure wasn't about money. Joe , riddled with guilt because the photo he sent to the newspapers may have led to Ned's death, finds himself embroiled in a dangerous game of who-dun-it that leads from L. A. 's Wrigley Field to an upscale sports bar in Altadena to the posh mansions of Pasadena and finally to the swank clubhouse of Santa Anita racetrack.

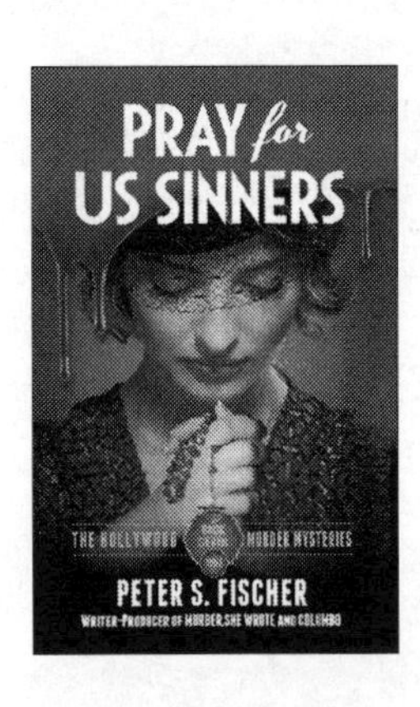

Book Seven—1953
PRAY FOR US SINNERS

Joe finds himself in Quebec but it's no vacation. Alfred Hitchcock is shooting a suspenseful thriller called "I Confess" and Montgomery Clift is playing a priest accused of murder. A marriage made in heaven? Hardly. They have been at loggerheads since Day One and to make matters worse their feud is spilling out into the newspapers. When vivacious Jeanne d'Arcy, the director of the Quebec Film Commisssion volunteers to help calm the troubled waters, Joe thinks his troubles are over but that was before Jeanne got into a violent spat with a former lover and suddenly found herself under arrest on a charge of first degree murder. Guilty or not guilty? Half the clues say she did it, the other half say she is being brilliantly framed. But by who? Fingers point to the crooked Gonsalvo brothers who have ties to the Buffalo mafia family and when Joe gets too close to the truth, someone tries to shut him up. . . permanently. With the Archbishop threatening to shut down the production in the wake of the scandal, Joe finds himself torn between two loyalties.

Book Eight–1954
HAS ANYBODY HERE SEEN WYCKHAM?

Everything was going smoothly on the set of "The High and the Mighty" until the cast and crew returned from lunch. With one exception. Wiley Wyckham, the bit player sitting in seat 24A on the airliner mockup, is among the missing, and without Wyckham sitting in place, director William Wellman cannot continue filming. A studio wide search is instituted. No Wyckham. A lookalike is hired that night, filming resumes the next day and still no Wyckham. Except that by this time, it's been discovered that Wyckham, a British actor, isn't really Wyckham at all but an imposter who may very well be an agent for the Russian government, The local police call in the FBI. The FBI calls in British counterintelligence. A manhunt for the missing actor ensues and Joe Bernardi, the picture's publicist, is right in the middle of the intrigue. Everyone's upset, especially John Wayne who is furious to learn that a possible Commie spy has been working in a picture he's producing and starring in. And then they find him . It's the dead of night on the Warner Brothers backlot and Wyckham is discovered hanging by his feet from a streetlamp, his body bloodied and tortured and very much dead. and pinned to his shirt is a piece of paper with the inscription "Sic Semper Proditor". (Thus to all traitors). Who was this man who had been posing as an obscure British actor? How did he smuggle himself into the country and what has he been up to? Has he been blackmailing an important higher-up in the film business and did the victim suddenly turn on him? Is the MI6 agent from London really who he says he is and what about the reporter from the London Daily Mail who seems to know all the right questions to ask as well all the right answers.

Book Nine—1955
EYEWITNESS TO MURDER

Go to New York? Not on your life. It's a lousy idea for a movie. A two year old black and white television drama? It hasn't got a prayer. This is the age of CinemaScope and VistaVision and stereophonic sound and yes, even 3-D. Burt Lancaster and Harold Hecht must be out of their minds to think they can make a hit movie out of "Marty". But then Joe Bernardi gets word that the love of his life, Bunny Lesher, is in New York and in trouble and so Joe changes his mind. He flies east to talk with the movie company and also to find Bunny and dig her out of whatever jam she's in. He finds that "Marty" is doing just fine but Bunny's jam is a lot bigger than he bargained for. She's being held by the police as an eyewitness to a brutal murder of a close friend in a lower Manhattan police station. Only a jammed pistol saved Bunny from being the killer's second victim and now she's in mortal danger because she knows what the man looks like and he's dead set on shutting her up. Permanently. Crooked lawyers, sleazy con artists and scheming businessmen cross Joe's path, determined to keep him from the truth and when the trail leads to the sports car racing circuit at Lime Rock in Connecticut, it's Joe who becomes the killer's prime target.

Book Ten—1956
A DEADLY SHOOT IN TEXAS

Joe Bernardi's in Marfa, Texas, and he's not happy. The tarantulas are big enough to carry off the cattle , the wind's strong enough to blow Marfa into New Mexico, and the temperature would make the Congo seem chilly. A few miles out of town Warner Brothers is shooting Edna Ferber's "Giant" with a cast that includes Rock Hudson, Elizabeth Taylor and James Dean and Jack Warner is paying through the nose for Joe's expertise as a publicist. After two days in Marfa Joe finds himself in a lonely cantina around midnight, tossing back a few cold ones, and being seduced by a gorgeous student young enough to be his daughter. The flirtation goes nowhere but the next morning little Miss Coed is found dead . And there's a problem. The coroner says she died between eight and nine o'clock. Not so fast, says Joe, who saw her alive as late as one a.m. When he points this out to the County Sheriff, all hell breaks loose and Joe becomes the target of some pretty ornery people. Like the Coroner and the Sheriff as well as the most powerful rancher in the county, his arrogant no-good son and his two flunkies, a crooked lawyer and a grieving father looking for justice or revenge, either one will do. Will Joe expose the murderer before the murderer turns Joe into Texas road kill? Tune in.

Book Eleven—1957
EVERYBODY LET'S ROCK

Big trouble is threatening the career of one of the country's hottest new teen idols and Joe Bernardi has been tapped to get to the bottom of it. Call it blackmail or call it extortion, a young woman claims that a nineteen year old Elvis Presley impregnated her and then helped arrange an abortion. There's a letter and a photo to back up her claim. Nonsense, says Colonel Tom Parker, Elvis's manager and mentor. It's a damned lie. Joe is not so sure but Parker is adamant. The accusation is a totally bogus and somebody's got to prove it. But no police can be involved and no lawyers. Just a whiff of scandal and the young man's future will be destroyed, even though he's in the midst of filming a movie that could turn him into a bona fide film star. Joe heads off to Memphis under the guise of promoting Elvis's new film and finds himself mired in a web of deceit and danger. Trusted by no one he searches in vain for the woman behind the letter, crossing paths with Sam Philips of Sun Records, a vindictive alcoholic newspaper reporter, a disgraced doctor with a seedy past, and a desperate con artist determined to keep Joe from learning the truth.

Book Twelve—1958
A TOUCH OF HOMICIDE

It takes a lot to impress Joe Bernardi. He likes his job and the people he deals with but nobody is really special. Nobody, that is, except for Orson Welles, and when Avery Sterling, a bottom feeding excuse for a producer, asks Joe's help in saving Welles from an industry-wide smear campaign, Joe jumps in, heedless that the pool he has just plunged into is as dry as a vermouthless martini. A couple of days later, Sterling is found dead in his office and the police immediately zero in on two suspects—Joe who has an alibi and Welles who does not. Not to worry, there are plenty of clues at the crime scene including a blood stained monogrammed handkerchief, a rejected screenplay, a pair of black-rimmed reading glasses, a distinctive gold earring and petals from a white carnation. What's more, no less than four people threatened to kill him in front of witnesses. A case so simple a two-year old could solve it but the cop on the case is a dimwit whose uncle is on the staff of the police commissioner. Will Joe and Orson solve the case before one of them gets arrested for murder? Will an out-of-town hitman kill one or both of them? Worst of all, will Orson leave town leaving Joe holding the proverbial bag?

FUTURE TITLES IN THE SERIES:

Some Like 'Em Dead
Dead Men Pay No Debts
The Death of Her Yet
Dead and Buried

Available in paperback or Kindle editions from Amazon.com

Made in the USA
Middletown, DE
19 August 2016